BLACKOUT GIRL

By Amber Leigh Larrain

To my family,

who supported me in my writing journey.

Prologue

March 2024

"The 'Blackout Girl' is in the interrogation room," a deep voice dripping with disdain said.

I could hear the sound of papers being shuffled and chatter in the distance.

"Pff!" laughed the other officer. "Is that what we are calling her now?"

My mind raced as they continued to talk. All I could hear was mumbling.

I sat at the cold table with my head in my hands, trying to block out as much as I could. The room was mostly empty, aside from three chairs, a table and a recording device in the center. This place was completely sterile—like I was in an insane asylum.

There was nothing in the room to distract me from every fiber of my being trying to scream out that I was not okay—palms sweating, whole body shaking, heart pounding. Nothing about this situation was okay.

A long exhale escaped my mouth. At this point, I was on autopilot, just trying to regulate my body before it became overwhelmed with anxiety. My mind was spinning, and I had no idea why I was here.

I hung on the precipice of going mad. Repeating to myself, *you are okay, you are okay* to keep myself right on the precipice—instead of deep diving off of it.

The two male officers who had been talking about me in the hallway walked in. Their footsteps were heavy, and each step pounded through me as they got closer, making me flinch over and over. Both men pulled out chairs and sat across from me, not taking their eyes off me as they did so.

The first officer was older and you could tell he had been handsome at some point, though age had puffed him out a bit now. The second officer was a young guy who must have been straight out of the police academy. He looked like the type to fly off the handle at any point. If he had been a woman, people would have said he had resting bitch face, but since he's a man, he's just authoritative.

The sternness of their faces unsettled me. I sensed they already had their minds made up about my guilt or innocence. I shifted in my seat trying to get more comfortable; a fruitless task.

Another long, slow exhale. *Keep it together, Isabella. This will all work out.* I kept repeating to myself, though I didn't believe it one bit.

The younger of the officers hit record on the device that sat on the table between us. "State your name for the record," he said with zero emotion in his voice as he stared at me.

"Isabella Frank."

"Today is Friday March 1, 2024. I am Officer Rossi and with me is Officer Clark, with the Hamilton Police Department. Miss Frank, let's start at the beginning. How did you know the victim?"

"What? What victim? Who are you talking about?"

"Don't play stupid with us. Tell us what happened tonight," said the old officer. His pudgy hands resting in his lap.

He was so smug. The way they looked at me, I could feel their distrust before I even opened my mouth. "I told you, I—"

"Blacked out," we all said in unison, their voices tinged with sarcasm.

Biting down on my lower lip, I could taste the tang of blood; metallic and warm. This wasn't going well and I had no idea how to make sense of it. I kept pulling at my sweatshirt as a coping mechanism, unaware of how skittish it made me look. Sure wasn't doing myself any favors.

While thoughts swirled in my head, I paused, trying to think of how to put it all together. I coughed and requested some water. A way to gain a few minutes and hopefully gain a sense of clarity.

The pudgy officer rose to get the water. While he was away, the younger one just glared at me. I had already forgotten both their names as all my mental energy was focused on decoding this situation.

Once I had the water in hand, I took a long swig. Though it only took seconds, time slowed down and it felt like an eternity before I continued.

"I woke up, laying on the ground. No memory of what happened. I was confused because I've never fallen asleep like that before," I lied. "The mental fog—it was like nothing I had ever experienced before. I looked around, trying to figure out where I was, when it was, why I was there. There was an incredible amount of confusion. And then I noticed the blood on the floor. It was everywhere. It was all too much." I gently closed my eyes. I needed a second to pause and regain my composure. "I was convinced that I was in a dream… a nightmare, I mean. Nothing about the situation made sense. I was either imagining it or going crazy."

The two officers side glanced at each other. It was as if they spoke to each other silently, as if they were saying, 'What a load of BS.'

My heart raced even faster. My muscles were stiff as a board. Realizing this uncomfortable sensation, I recalled what my therapist said and I slowly released the tension muscle by muscle. This only helped relax me a bit. If I couldn't get them to believe me now, I didn't know what I would do.

"You stated you felt like you were going crazy. Do you often feel like you're going crazy? Like you can't control your emotions?" Officer Rossi asked me.

Their accusations caused a lightning bolt of anger to pulse through me. I ran my fingers through my dark brown hair in the hopes of self-soothing, but there was a cold gooey feeling on my fingers as I did so.

"Dammit! I didn't hurt anyone!" I barked as I slammed my hand on the table. When I lifted my hand, all that hung between us was silence… and the bloody imprint of my hand.

Chapter 1

5 Months Earlier, November 2023

I sat slumped in the chair of my apartment.
I was hollow.
Just a shell of a person.

It felt as if each limb was filled with sacks of sand and every move required far more energy than I could muster. I couldn't explain how I got to this place in my life, but I wasn't functioning; and that fact would just cause me to spiral even more.

For the past three months, I'd been having episodes of deep sadness and then it would fade, only to return days later.

People around me would tell me to, 'Smile more.' The amount of times I was told something that oversimplified and dismissed what I was dealing with was unreal.

My family doctor didn't give me any useful advice. I was sent to a host of other doctors but no progress was made. After all the time, energy, and money put in, I was no better off than when I started. The frustration and hopelessness pulled my mental health down like an anchor on a boat.

For the fourth time, my alarm sounded and I glared at my phone with hatred; as if I wasn't the one who had set it go off. My first thought was to slap the snooze again, but if I didn't leave now, I'd be late.

Every ounce of energy I had was used to get myself through the door, in the car, and on my way.

I parked my car in front of my therapist's office. I gripped onto the steering wheel and rested my head on top of my hands. I sat there for several minutes trying to steal away a moment and settle myself before the appointment.

The sign on the door read Danielle Price, Licensed Clinical Professional Counselor. The bell chimed as I walked through it, which, as always, set off this dual rush of emotions. I felt obligated to come to deal with all my emotional baggage, but terrified of continuing to release my full range of emotions, insecurities and oddities to someone who was essentially a stranger.

The smell of lavender wafted through her office, a calming scent that I enjoyed. It did help to ease my nerves a bit. She flicked on the white noise machine that sat just outside the door to the room where she met with clients, to give privacy in case the next client arrived early.

"Isabella!" she greeted me warmly. "Please sit down." She waved her hand, motioning towards the large armchair.

Danielle Price was girl-next-door beautiful. She always dressed stylishly, but never in a way that seemed forced or over the top. She walked towards her chair, her black slacks hugging every curve and her black four inch heals clicking lightly on the wooden floor. Her multicolored silk top was mesmerizing. She had swept her dark blonde hair into a casual updo.

What always caught my eye was the huge engagement ring that she wore above her wedding ring. It was so large that I found it distracting. It was a bit over the top, but that was probably my own jealousy speaking. I was twenty-four and hadn't ever had a serious relationship. I decided to stuff my jealousy down. There were bigger things I needed to work on.

I took a deep inhale and sat on the warm brown leather seat. I glanced around at the same photos I'd been looking at for the last year. Maybe it was boredom, but I read the inspirational quotes on them over and over, despite the fact that I thought they were bullshit. The room was minimally decorated but had a warmth to it.

"Where should we start today? How have you coped this week?" Her voice was calm like an ASMR video.

Long, slow exhale. What should I say? What do I leave out? "Well…" I paused. Then my phone chirped. It was facing up, intentionally, as I was waiting to hear from someone. I glanced to read the partial message hoping it was from Christian. It was.

Christian: **Hello gorgeous. Are we still on for tonight?**

The smile that spread across my face was clearly noticeable as Dr. Price commented that it was good to see me smile. I avoided saying anything in response. What could I say? Things with Christian were complicated and I wasn't exactly sure where we stood.

"My week has been- subpar," I admitted. "I want to do things I enjoy. I want to connect with my friends and family. I want to have energy. But I just don't." My voice was full of self-pity and feeling embarrassed from my pity party, I tried to self-correct.

I had never been depressed in the past, so all this was new to me. However, since this fog of depression hit me, it has been weaving in and out of my life. The weight of it, the instability; it was foreign to the happy and healthy person I had been. It was my top priority to get back to that person. Hopefully, she wasn't gone forever.

"Well, let's start with what went well. Clearly, something is able to put a smile on your face."

I modified my voice to sound more chipper than I felt. "I met someone…" I began, trying to mimic the giddiness of a girl with a love interest. At this point, though, there wasn't much to tell.

Christian had messaged me through a dating app that I thought I had deactivated. Right now was probably the worst time to start dating, all things considered. When I first got the notification, I was about to ignore it… until I saw his face. It was strikingly handsome. He had tanned skin and wavy black hair. He was toned in a way that showed he tried to keep fit, but didn't live at the gym. However, what made me decide to message back was his bright green eyes. I was a sucker for a pretty set of eyes.

We had gone out twice so far for coffee. He said all the right things and looks-wise, he was definitely my type. Our conversations, with some minor flirting, flowed smoothly but these dates hadn't led to anything more than conversation. His jokes made me laugh and he had a way about him; I just enjoyed his company.

Despite this, I had reservations about him. He had canceled last-minute on one of our planned dates last week. Sometimes he seemed like he was distracted, other times totally focused on me. I couldn't completely figure him out at this point. There was a lot I needed to learn about him to see if we were a good fit or not.

Dr. Price listened as I spoke and then asked, "So far, do you feel there is a good rapport? Is this person respectful to you? And considerate of what you are experiencing now?"

I tilted my head, considering her question. "Mostly."

"Say more." She always said this and it mildly irked me. I'd have said more if I wanted to say more.

I expressed how Christian was sometimes distracted. He'd check his phone throughout our time together, which I thought was pretty rude, especially as we were just getting to know each other. The phone constantly chirped, interjecting into our conversations like a small child needing attention. He also seemed like he was pushing me to hang out tonight even though I said I had no energy. Those things aside, which I realize were quite a few things so early on in a potential relationship, I was enjoying our time together.

"Anyone you let into your life should be respectful of your boundaries, Isabella. Make it clear what you are and are not comfortable with and only open yourself up to people who are going to care for you in the way you deserve."

I agreed. It was time to put my needs first. The last few months had been the most difficult of my life. Processing the loss of my friend and then the debilitating depression was more than enough to deal with right now. I wasn't going to complicate it with a messy romance.

I left that session feeling confused about what to do next. Was dating Christian going to lead to a complicated relationship or would we just need to work out some issues as we got to know each other?

Was Christian out of line? Or was I finding issues in order to push him away?

I had done this before, so I decided I needed to reframe my issues with Christian. Going forward, I had to have a more positive perspective. Many people were on their phones all the time, I told myself. As for pushing me to hang out, it wasn't that he wasn't being empathic to my situation, he just wanted to be with me.

That was a good thing.

Chapter 2

I pulled up the message on my phone and reread it.

Christian: **Hello gorgeous. Are we still on for tonight?**

He had added a heart emoji after it fifteen minutes later when I didn't respond.

I began to type: **Sorry I was in a meeting. I'll see you around eight? Same coffee shop?**

The three little dots indicating he was typing appeared on my screen. Excitement bubbled up in me. I was looking forward to staring into those green eyes again. This could be a chance to understand him better and to see if I wanted to explore where this relationship would take us.

The phone chirped.

Christian: **How about I come to your place?**

I was not expecting that. How did I feel about this? Did I want things to move along? Was this too fast?

Sure, I typed with my finger hovering over the send button. I thought for a moment more and then pushed send.

Christian: **Text me your address. I'll see you soon, Gorgeous.**

Quickly, I began to clean my house as best I could. The mound of unopened mail that laid on my coffee table was swept into a bag and tossed into my closet. I pushed the dirty clothes on my bathroom floor into the linen closet. The place could now pass for being clean, as long as he didn't stumble upon any of my piles of stuff I'd deal with later. I put just as much effort into getting myself ready—a quick run through my hair with a brush and a swipe of mascara.

8:00 pm arrived and went. Perhaps I was being stood up. Wouldn't be the first time, I thought glumly. My mind bounced from one extreme to another. First, my thoughts went from being worried that perhaps he was in an accident. Then they bounced to angered that he couldn't bother to send a quick text that he couldn't make it tonight. As the minutes ticked by, I became more convinced. After thirty-five minutes had passed, I decided to just go to bed.

As I was pulling myself up, my doorbell rang. The melodic sound clashed with my foul mood. There was Christian standing at my door looking neither sorry nor embarrassed.

"Well, thanks for showing up," I tried to say sarcastically but ended up sounding petty.

"Sorry, Gorgeous. I got caught up at work."

"Call next time," I said firmly. Setting boundaries was important—or so my therapist said.

"Noted," he replied to me with a wink and a smile.

It was like I had a Banana Republic model standing in front of me with his ivory sweater that gently hugged his muscular arms, and jeans that were tight in just the right places. I felt a little self-conscious in my PINK sweats and high ponytail. He reached for my hand and despite trying to stay angry, I smiled at the sweet gesture.

I moved in such a way to allow him to enter, silently forgiving him. He walked into my place with confidence like he had been there before. I offered him a drink and he followed me into the kitchen.

He immediately noticed my collection of magnets on the black refrigerator. "Are all those from places you've been to?" he asked, impressed as he walked towards it.

"Yes." I tried to sound casual. I love the fact that I had the opportunity to travel but always felt a bit elitist when people found out to what extent. Travel is always seen as a luxury, but the way I traveled was anything but luxurious.

"So, how many countries have you been to?" He began to pick certain magnets off the refrigerator to examine them before replacing it and moving on to the next.

"Forty-two," I replied.

He raised his eyebrows and paused before putting back the Norway magnet with little cartoonish Vikings in a wooden boat. "Seriously? That's pretty awesome. I've been to three... no, four if you count Canada."

"I count it." I smiled at him. He was just so handsome.

"People always think travel has to be expensive, but I never had money growing up. I saved a lot over a few summers work. It was enough to spend a few weeks traveling around Europe—staying in hostels, making a lot of my meals. It's possible if you are willing to rough it a bit."

"I'd rather not cook on vacation and I think I'm a little too old for hostels at this point."

Christian was thirty-five. Not old, but some might say he aged out of the hostels, which were mostly filled with college-aged students.

"There is always Air B&B's, old man."

Christian laughed and then he took my hand and led me to my couch. I felt butterflies in anticipation of what I knew was coming next. I stopped halfway and turned back to the kitchen to get some wine. I poured two glasses halfway with some cheap white wine that I had in my refrigerator.

"Hope you like two buck chuck," I said, handing him his glass.

He looked at me and then at the wine, considering the situation, a half-smile peeking out.

"What?" I asked playfully.

"I just assumed a girl who has been all over Europe might have fancier taste in wine."

I laughed. "Well, I probably would if my bank account would let me. Working for a non-profit doesn't pay big bucks. But next time you take me out, you're welcome to get us a nice bottle." I winked at him.

"Deal," he quickly agreed. "So, what is your favorite place you've been to?" His phone chirped and he apologized as he completely shut it down. I made a mental note that this was a good sign and maybe all my concerns were overblown.

Feeling bold, I sat right next to him on the small couch so our legs touched. I took a gulp of my wine. It was so bland that it was hard to swallow. "It's hard to pick a favorite! The landscape in Scandinavia is breathtaking. The food and art in France is what draws me back there."

I had more to say but I thought I'd stop before I sounded like too much of a snob. I tried to direct the conversation back to him to take the spotlight off me—a place I was never comfortable to be in. "So, what is a place you'd like to travel to?"

He thought for a moment. "I haven't really thought about it. Work has always been so crazy and I don't really have anyone to travel with."

Christian had told me he worked in advertising in the city but I didn't know much more about it. I know it was early in the relationship but I wanted him to see me as someone he could have a future with. I'd eagerly travel anywhere with this man.

He leaned into me so close that I could feel the warmth from his breath. His eyes locked on mine. Christian had a confidence about him that must have developed from emerging from his twenties unscathed.

"But if you wanted to join me, I'd be happy to go anywhere sunny with a beach. Maybe Jamaica or Belize. I just want a beautiful beach, cocktails, a hammock and warm weather."

"I'd love that. You'd have to hold my hand on the flight, though. As much as I've traveled, I've never seemed to overcome a pretty intense fear of flying."

"I hear you. Being up that high, at the mercy of two pilots you've never met can be a little nerve-wracking. It's completely safe but I'll hold your hand and make you feel better."

I couldn't help but smile at that. There were no awkward pauses in our conversation. It all felt so very natural. Being with him felt really good and that was foreign to me.

"Okay, so after traveling so much. Where would be the best place to live?" he asked me.

"New Jersey."

He nearly spit out his wine from laughing so hard. My face was totally deadpan. "Oh… you are serious?"

"Hell yeah," I said, knowing there was no one more New Jersey than me. I had grown up here and even after seeing a good part of the world, I thought this was the best place to settle.

"So, you are going to need to explain this to me." He smirked.

"You better get ready, Christian. I have a whole spiel. So here in central New Jersey, you have it all. You are an hour from two major cities. Some people wait their whole life to travel to New York City but we could go there for dinner. You could also do a day trip to Washington DC. We are forty minutes from the beach and also have farmlands everywhere. An Ivy League school just up the road. We have a ton of major airports so it makes traveling the world easier. And we don't have to pump our own gas."

"So basically, heaven on Earth."

"Not basically. It is!" I said confidently.

"Okay, well, I'll be sure to deny any transfers if my company wants me to go to Paris, France. I'll say screw your delicious croissants. I need easy access to the turnpike."

I playfully hit his arm and then he pulled me in and the whole world went into slow motion. Christian's hand slipped through my hair and pulled me towards him. He gently kissed me with his soft lips. The taste of the cheap wine on his mouth met mine. I pulled away to admire how handsome he was. Wanting more, we placed our wine glasses on the table and gravitated toward each other like magnets. Our hands began wandering desperately as the kiss intensified.

When he did pull away from me, he smirked. "You're pretty amazing."

I smiled back, keeping hidden the rush of emotion.

It amazed me how different you can feel about yourself by the company you are surrounded with. I'd been on dates that had zero chemistry. All my jokes fell flat and the lack of connection made me not only feel awkward about the situation, but about myself.

On the flip side, you could be with someone who everything clicks into place. All your jokes are hilarious and they can quip right back with you and send you into uncontrollable laughter. Everything you say is genuinely interesting to them and you are fully engaged with everything they add to the conversation. The connection makes you feel like a better you.

That is how this felt. Easy. Comfortable. Enjoyable.

Christian looked around the small living room and I watched him as he did so. He walked over to the wooden bookshelves that filled one full wall of my living room. There was something that caught his eye and he picked up a photo propped between books. A few of the books toppled over which didn't seem to phase him.

"Is this when you were younger?" he said, pointing to one of the two young girls in the photo.

"No," I said sadly as I readjusted the fallen books. "That's me." I pointed to the other girl.

"So, who is the other girl?"

"That's…" My voice cracked. When would I be able to talk about this? I paused and collected myself. "That is… was my friend Aubrey. We became friends in first grade."

Christian put his hand on the small of my back and a rush of comfort enveloped me.

"You don't need to say more if you don't want to."

I forced a smile to convey that I was okay. It was a lie.

"I used to see a therapist who was always asking me to 'say more', which was very annoying so I appreciate that you think that," I said with a half-hearted laugh.

I shouldn't have lied, but people had stigmas about therapy. Despite the fact I was dealing with this trauma, I wanted him to think I was okay. Christian had furrowed his eyebrows like I had said something odd.

"Aubrey was my best friend. She... we were in a car accident a few months ago and she passed away. I miss her every day... and, of course, I have this overwhelming guilt because I am here and she is not. It hits me for all the little things, like today I get to make my morning coffee, but Aubrey can not. Or when I am caught in traffic and I want to be angry but then realize I'm lucky to even have this time. It makes you appreciate each moment you have, but also be so devastated that these precious moments were stolen from her."

Tears were now pooling in my eyes and soon my head was buried in his shoulder. His arms wrapped around me. Grief is difficult because people move on, go on with their lives and you have to pretend you're living too. At first, everyone is all over you. You get a hundred messages asking how you are and everyone wants to send you prepared meals to reheat alone on your couch. Your grief makes them a little too uncomfortable to sit there and eat it with you.

Two weeks or so after, people stopped asking how I felt; how I was doing. No more offers to help out. You are standing still, frozen in grief while the world keeps bustling around you, perplexed as to why you aren't moving too. So, I hadn't spoken about the pain of this to anyone in a long time, but of course I still carried it. I'd always carry it. Aubrey's death was on my mind all the time and the grief was like a boa constrictor squeezing the life out of me.

I needed to talk about this. We sat together on my couch just talking until midnight. He nodded his head as I spoke and kept eye contact with me, fully engaged and supportive as I spilled my heart out.

Late into the night, I let out a big yawn, unable to hide my sleepiness. "Sorry, this night probably wasn't what you were expecting."

"No need to apologize. We all need someone to listen to us."

"Well, that's what therapy is for," I quipped, hoping he'd chuckle. "I don't do that anymore though," I lied again.

"I never met a therapist I liked. Most of them probably get into the field because they have their own shit to work through. Sometimes it's just better to vent to a good listener," he responded stoically.

He gently kissed my forehead and I looked up and pulled him into one last kiss goodnight.

"I'll see you soon," he said as he looked at me for one last moment before turning to leave.

I closed the door behind him and pressed my back to the wooden panel. I shut my eyes, absorbing all the magic that was floating around me and thought that I couldn't wait to see him again.

Wherever this was heading, I was all in for it.

Chapter 3

I woke up the next morning with the sun shining through my window, waking me way before I wanted to get up.

"Too early! Too early!" I complained to no one. I groggily reached for my phone and saw that in fact it was not too early. It was 10:30 am. I scrolled through the several notifications: texts from my mother, texts from Christian and an automated reminder that I had a session with Dr. Price in two days.

Mom: **How are you, my love? I wanted to come visit this weekend—preferably today. Please let me know a good time to stop by.**

Mom: **Don't mean to bother, but just want to see if you are okay. Love you.**

Christian: **Good morning Gorgeous. Thank you for sharing your story with me. I'd love to see you again.**

I tossed the phone onto the empty space on the comforter, closed the curtains and went back into my warm bed. The blanket was pulled around me creating a cocoon to block out the world. Being alone and blocking out the world was my comfort zone.

When I woke again, I checked my phone to see:

Mom: **Please respond. Just want to know you are okay, my love.**

Mom: **If you see this and are busy, please just give it a thumbs up so I know all is well.**

Mom: **Please. Don't mean to pester you…but I'm worried.**

Mom: **Isabella?**

Mom: **Isabella?!**

As I read, there was a loud knock at my door. The clock said 2:00 pm. I'd slept half the day away yet still felt tired. The knocking continued becoming louder and faster. Unsure of what I'd find on the other side, I slowly crept towards the door.

"Bella!" a voice semi-frantic called through the door. The only one who calls me Bella is my mother.

When I opened the door a look of pure relief washed over her face. She didn't need to say it. I knew what she was thinking.

"I was sleeping," I explained.

She shoved a large box of pastries into my hand, causing the smell of fresh baked sweets to fill my nose. "I bought these earlier today. Before the panic set in."

I thank her as I take the box. For a second, if I closed my eyes, I could have been back in Paris. The label on the box indicated that they were from my favorite shop. Normally, the sight of these would have me drooling, but I had no desire to eat.

She forced a smile that looked like it weighed on her. It was the smile that could only come from someone worn down and tired with constant worry. I gestured for her to sit down on the couch in my living room. She made a few minutes of small talk before moving on to what I called her Motherly Assessment portion of the visit.

"How have your therapy sessions been going?" she asked cautiously.

I knew this was a difficult situation for her; to see her child in pain, to worry about what was next for me, always worrying if my long response time meant I'd done something final and would never respond again. While I felt empathy for her, it still didn't make her questions any less annoying to me as I was stood there fine albeit sleepy.

"Fine, I guess. She's nice enough. Sometimes a bit unprofessional."

"What do you mean?"

"She always has her phone out. She'll sometimes text as I am speaking. But to be fair, I haven't really mentioned that it makes me uncomfortable."

"You pay a lot of money for this so you should feel comfortable with who you are seeing." She took a long pause before continuing. "Do you think it might be time to switch to a psychiatrist? Maybe talking with someone isn't enough… maybe it's time to meet with someone who can also prescribe medication."

"Mom, we've been over this. At this point, I really don't want to start with someone new. It takes a long time to build a rapport with someone and besides, I'd rather not be on medication just yet."

I was desperate to change the conversation. For both of our sakes, we needed to move on to a new topic. So, I threw out the topic that I knew would hook her. "I met someone," I blurted out.

A genuine smile spread across her face, this time raising her cheekbones and highlighting the small lines around her eyes. Then she raised her eyebrows. "Oh, Bella, that's great news! Tell me all about him."

She was lovely when she smiled despite the wrinkles that showed around her eyes when she did so. She propped her elbows on her knees and leaned into me as I spoke as if we were friends ready for girl talk. I liked when we were in this mode, rather than the previous one.

"His name is Christian. We've been out three times so far. We are still getting to know each other but he is kind, funny and so handsome. He has these gorgeous green eyes that are so striking you'd almost think they weren't real."

My mother gently placed her hand on my knee. "I'm so happy for you. I'll say a little prayer that it continues to go well." My mother wasn't particularly religious but she prayed when she wanted something positive to happen.

I put my hand on top of hers. My life had been rather reclusive lately and the touch of another person made me feel comforted.

I could tell she wanted to say something. "What?" I asked.

"Bella, I just want you to know. You are more than what you are experiencing now. You are this whole person who has had so many rich experiences and influenced so many people's lives positively. Sometimes I think you lose sight of that.

"When you were little, you played the flute in third grade as you know, and I put the music your teacher gave as homework in front of you and you played it beautifully. So, I found something harder, and again you played that beautifully too. And this continued on and on. I was in awe of this little person who couldn't find a musical obstacle. This little person who took a cylinder of metal and made me weep with the beauty they created. There was such a light in you when you played. You sparkled Bella. You still have that spark in you and to me you still sparkle. Even on days and moments you don't see it."

I was speechless.

Chapter 4

After my mother left, I thought about what she said. I knew I couldn't magically make myself better, but I could try to work on the healing process. Then and there, I vowed to do more research into what I was experiencing to understand it better. The path I was on was unsustainable and I was determined to make an effort to improve my mental health.

I pulled out my phone to reply to Christian: **I'd love to see you again too. When are you free?**

I stared at the message for a bit. Maybe I'd play it a bit cooler. I deleted '**When are you free?**' and pressed send. I'd let him try to set up the next meet up.

Surprisingly, I had some energy for the first time in a few days. I walked around my place picking up dirty dishes that had accumulated over days, maybe even weeks. All the dirty clothes I had stashed in the closet were tossed into the washing machine. I even started to tackle the unopened mail, which was a taunting task at this point. Until my energy ran out, I was going to get my home looking like it should.

Thirty minutes later the living room and kitchen looked noticeably cleaner. I could feel myself relax more with the clutter removed. While I normally had zero desire to clean, I did get satisfaction out of being in a clean space.

My phone chirped.

Christian: **Hello Gorgeous. I'm free tomorrow night. Let's get dinner this time.**

Me: **I'd like that.**

We worked out the details to meet through several texts back and forth. Some flirting on his end but I was being coy.

Four dates.

That was getting to be serious. Definitely the most serious I've been since my first year of college, as I hadn't had much luck with dating previously. Would this make him my boyfriend? I thought to myself.

Christian picked me up the next night. He wore stylish jeans with a brown leather belt and a navy polo shirt. He looked incredibly handsome. He hadn't told me where we were going so I was pleased that what I wore, a little black dress and black ballerina flats, matched with his vibe. My dark brown hair was pulled up into a bun.

My date walked out of my apartment building with his hand lightly cupping the small of my back. His touch sent shivers through my body. He opened the door to a new silver Audi convertible. Since every penny I ever earned went to travel, I'd never been in a car this nice and this was all starting to feel like I didn't belong here. He flipped on the radio to play soft jazz. The relaxing notes put me at ease.

As we drove to the restaurant, he'd glance at me when we stopped at red lights and I'd melt. We drove for thirty minutes and conversation flowed smoothly.

We were led to a table that overlooked the Delaware River. He pulled out my chair and I placed my small black clutch on the white tablecloth.

"Looks like a place where I won't be able to pronounce what I want to order."

He chuckled in response. "Somehow I don't believe that." He pulled out my chair and then sat down across from me. He looked around the restaurant. "I've been here a few times. The food is low-key but delicious. I owe you a nice bottle of wine, don't I?"

"You sure do," I said smiling at him.

When the waiter arrived to ask about our drink order, Christian asked for a bottle of his nicest white wine.

As we looked over the menus his phone kept buzzing but he never picked it up. He seemed slightly pained every time it went off. After the sixth or seventh buzz, he powered it down.

"You're popular tonight!" I mused, hoping he might open up about it.

"I'm popular every night," he quipped back, and I laughed.

The waiter arrived, poured a splash of white wine into each of our cups. We swirled and swigged. The floral and fruity notes danced on my tongue. Then we nodded in approval and the waiter filled each glass full.

Once our dinners arrived our conversation slowed while we ate. We ordered different dishes. I had the cod with green beans and a baked potato. He had the mushroom risotto. Both plates looked delicious and we ended up splitting them. Both our wine glasses had emptied and he reached to refill them.

"So, Mr. Popular, tell me something I don't know about you?" I said flirtatiously as I went for a spoonful of his risotto. He pushed the bowl towards me to make it easier.

"I'm married."

I glared at him, waiting for a smirk but none came. I tilted my head to the side. "Very funny," I said dryly.

He sighed. "I'm not, unfortunately. I wasn't sure how to tell you—and this probably wasn't the best way. I've been separated for over two years. My ex hasn't been able to cope with it ending and hasn't finalized the divorce. It's been hell."

"Jesus, Christian," I snapped, feeling the effects of the wine making me bolder. "That's not how the game is played! You're supposed to say something quirky like, 'I still wear superhero underwear' or, 'I'd really prefer a pet raccoon over a dog', not drop a huge bomb on me. You should have disclosed this before we met!" As some heads turned toward me, I lowered my voice so the other diners didn't hear me. "I don't want to date a married man!"

He slowly ran his palm over his face and sighed deeply.

"And I don't want to be a married man. I wish you could see this from my perspective. When things were first falling apart, she kept threatening to hurt herself so I'd stay. Eventually, I did leave. We have not intentionally spent time together in over two years, aside from legal meetings. She's got me in this limbo. I can't leave her because she won't sign the papers. I can't fully move on because, as you pointed out, no one wants to date a married man with a seriously complicated situation."

I raised my hand to my mouth and began to bite at my nails, a nervous habit I had never kicked. This night quickly went from being blissful to giving me major anxiety.

Based on every Lifetime movie I'd ever seen, I should assume that he is actually a happily married man who was going to string me along for the next several years until I snap and kill him. But what if he was telling the truth? If so, he could use someone to support him.

"Come on, Eeeeh-saaah," he cooed.

This was the first time he had used a nickname for me and I found it endearing. He powered the cellphone back up, entered his passcode and handed me the device. He gave me free rein to look through. On the main screen, I could see twelve unread texts from 'Crazy'.

I handed it back, satisfied that if he had nothing to hide, I would just trust him. "I assume those texts are from your ex."

He laughed dryly. "Yeah, it used to say something worse but my mother saw it and reprimanded me. 'I raised you better than that!' she said and so I changed it."

Our waiter returned asking how everything was going. *Not exactly as I had planned*, was what I wanted to say but since I knew he was asking about the food I replied, "Lovely, thank you."

He offered to bring the dessert menu but I quickly declined for the both of us.

As the waiter placed the check directly in front of Christian, I threw back what was left of my wine and then leaned across the table towards him.

"Christian Sandoval, you better be telling me the truth or I'm going to kill you," I said casually.

"Understood." With that, I reached for his hand and my decision was made.

Chapter 5

At my next therapy session, I felt relieved as I walked in. The familiar chirp as I entered, followed by that beautiful smell of lavender. A string of good moments had preceded this visit and I was feeling hopeful.

"Hello, Isabella. Please sit down," Dr. Price said softly.

I sat in the familiar chair.

"Would you like something to drink?"

I accepted a bottle of water which she popped the cap off before handing it over.

"So how have you been managing since we last met?" Her phone buzzed and she glanced over at it. I tried hard not to roll my eyes.

"I've had several good days. My energy level was normal. It was nice to be able to get some chores done around the house and to go out too. I was able to buy a few holiday gifts."

Her face changed as she read the message on her phone and I couldn't make out her emotion but I assumed it wasn't positive. It took her a beat to respond to me.

"Good to hear! You were able to go out with friends?"

"No," I replied. "With a date actually. We've gone out four times now. He's a very nice guy but I do have some worries."

"Why's that?"

"Well…" I was a bit embarrassed to discuss the situation. I didn't want my therapist to think I was doing something immoral but I also wanted to hear her opinion. "Like I said, he is very kind. He is a good listener and very attentive. On our last date though, he told me he was married… well, separated."

Dr. Price's had been writing on her notepad but at the word married she lifted her head up. "Married?" She raised her eyebrows and looked at me with her head tilted.

I didn't know what I expected her to say or do, but I felt self-conscious. Dating a married man was wrong and despite knowing this, I had decided to continue seeing Christian. A mixture of embarrassment and defensiveness tumbled from my mouth.

"Well, he's not really married. He's been estranged from his wife, for a while now."

I tried to talk quickly to fill in the gaps so that she could see what I see—a person who is in a bad situation;

locked into a marriage only because his ex won't let him go. Not some creep out cheating on his loving wife! I explained everything he had told me on our previous date. She didn't look convinced.

"He is a good man," I added.

Again, she quickly looked up at me, but this time her eyes were narrowed.

"Isabella, you are in a very delicate situation now. Most therapists would tell you to hold off on trying to go through the dating process at this time. And then to add in that this person is married." She softened her voice in a motherly way and looked at me sympathetically. "This isn't what you need right now... speaking as your therapist."

"He told me that he is waiting for the divorce papers to be signed. She means nothing to him at this point other than being a total nuisance in his life. He wants to move on... and I think he wants to move on with me by his side." I sounded like a child arguing with their parents.

She glared at me while tapping her pen on her notepad. "You *need* to do what is best for you and you *need* to focus on your mental health right now. Isabella, you've been through a lot in the past few months. I think it is best if you focus on that."

"Okay, I suppose you are right," I agreed, not meaning a word of it. "I don't know what I was thinking. Things have been so difficult lately that I suppose I just liked his attention but I need to be with someone stable. I'll end it."

She smiled and whispered, "It is what is best for you."

We moved on to other topics for the rest of the session; my upcoming return to work; issues in my social life; my lack of energy and non-existent appetite. I told her how some days were fine and some I could sit in the same spot for nearly the whole day. She listened and wrote, as she always did. At the end, I told her I'd see her next week for my joint session with my mother.

I walked out of her office once our fifty minutes were up, with an unsettled feeling. Obviously, most people would discourage you from dating someone with this messy circumstance but she didn't seem to see my side of it. Because of that, I had to lie to her about my intentions. Definitely not what I'd want out of a therapy session.

It was late and I hadn't eaten anything all day. My stomach rumbled and I was thankful to have some of my appetite back. I decided to go quickly and get a triple cheeseburger, milkshake and large fries. I sat with my food and scrolled on my phone. A friend request popped up on Facebook: Christian Sandoval would like to be your friend! I clicked accept and was given access to all his posts. After popping a few fries into my mouth, I scrolled through. No hint of a wife or worse, a full secret family.

Obviously, he could have two Facebook accounts but these photos went back years and years. There was engagement with each of the photos from what seemed like different friends and family. It seemed legitimate to me and that put me a bit more at ease.

His most recent post said it was from a holiday work party, taken a week ago. He was dressed up and looked amazing with his jet-black hair slicked back. He stood with several coworkers, some in Santa hats, casually smiling on a balcony that overlooked New York City. They all had champagne flutes in their hands. I gave it a thumbs up and then commented, 'Happy Holidays!' I spent the next fifteen minutes alternating between eating and scrolling.

Chapter 6

The next morning, the fog returned and I couldn't get out of bed. I looked at my phone. Two messages, both from Christian.

Christian: **Hey Gorgeous, are you my new Facebook stalker?**

Then forty-five minutes later when I didn't respond:

Christian: **Sorry, was that in poor taste? Anyway, how about we hang out tomorrow?**

Up to this point, I had managed to hide my ups and downs, but if we were going to continue seeing each other, I couldn't keep this from him. Revealing you have any ailment—physical or mental is always a risk. Even the most sympathetic people don't want to hear about your illness often, they quickly become tired of your cancelations, your excuses, your long stories about how you are feeling.

Your illness, and all that comes with it, is an inconvenience for them. 'Why can't you just be well? Why can't you just be normal?' It is never said, but always felt in the way they start to message you less, 'forget' to invite you to something. The whole experience, when you need people most, quickly becomes very isolating.

I typed back: **I'm not doing so well today. I've got no energy. I just woke up and I think I may go back to bed for another few hours.**

Christian: **Do you have the flu? Or Covid? I can bring you something—medicine or food if you'd like.**

I typed back: **Thank you. I didn't catch anything. I've been having episodes of depression for a few months now.**

He didn't reply for several minutes so I laid my head down and when I woke again, it was three hours later.

A message from Christian had come in that read: **Let me know how I can best help you. I can just sit with you in silence, just hold your hand, talk with you or give you space. I want to be there in the way you need me.**

A looked at the phone in stunned silence and then surprised myself by falling back into my pillow and audibly sobbing.

On my bad days I was always told to just cheer up, just smile, everything will be fine. His message made me feel seen, validated. It was the first time someone's response to my issues felt genuine and helpful. Like they actually cared.

His response showed so much kindness and reminded me there was someone in my life who deserved that same treatment—Talia.

I arranged to meet with my childhood friend later that night.

Talia, Aubrey and I had been friends since we were little. I had basically been avoiding her since the night Aubrey died. She had reached out many, many, times. Sure, I responded but always had an excuse for why I couldn't meet up. In the days and weeks after, I was positive that spending time together would be too awkward, too painful. My thoughts on it had started to evolve. Maybe we could find comfort in each other's company… as long as she didn't think I was responsible for Aubrey's death.

I walked into the pizza joint and saw Talia already sitting at our table. The table we had spent so many nights at after school; our parents' money wrinkled in our pockets just waiting to be spent on a slice of pizza and a can of soda.

When she looked up at me, I instantly knew everything would be okay.

She looked happy to see me. What a relief. The tension held in my shoulders began to release and I felt myself go into a more natural, less rigid posture.

A steaming hot pizza with onion and garlic was placed on the table along with two Dr. Peppers.

"I got the toppings you like. I joked with them that if there wasn't enough garlic to keep vampires away, we'd send it back," she said.

"As always, I came prepared," I said dropping a pack of mint gum on the table. The comfort and familiarity of a long friendship showed in this simple moment.

I grabbed a slice, watching the steam twirl like a ballerina above it. We started with small talk—work, the weather. We were dancing around the topic we both knew she wanted to get to and that I was dreading.

"So…I wanted to talk to you about that night," Talia started slowly, twisting her long black hair tightly around her finger. Shit, this wasn't exactly the place to have a serious conversation.

"Tal, can we not do this here? Let's just… eat," I pleaded somewhat pathetically as I took a large bite of the pizza.

"How much longer can we pretend this didn't happen? It's healing to talk through these things. We both loved her, both miss her." Her voice cracked at the end.

"Don't you think I know that? I can't do this now, not here, not today," I insisted. "I can't do this with you in a pizza shop of all places."

Talia bit her lower lip. Tears started lining her eyes and her mascara began to blur. I handed her a napkin to wipe them away. I really couldn't handle this right now, right here.

"Listen, why don't you come over tomorrow night. It will be private and I won't have been so blindsided by it. I want to be there for you, I really do, Tal. I just wasn't expecting to talk about this tonight. Please understand."

She nodded her head and then wiped at her eyes again, denying her tears the chance to flow down her reddened face. I filled the silence by adding, "I'll see you tomorrow. We will talk tomorrow, I promise."

Chapter 7

The next night Talia arrived at my house. I had spent the day mentally preparing for this. Despite that, I probably still wasn't ready to have this conversation but a promise is a promise.

"Do you want something to drink? Wine? Beer?" I offered and then instantly regretted it. I quickly added, "Water, Coffee, Tea?"

"I'm fine," Talia said.

Well, this was it. I really couldn't put it off any longer.

I looked uncomfortably down at my feet as each part of me became jittery. "So... Tal, I just don't even know what to say. You know I'm sorry." I looked up at her. She was already crying and I slipped my hand around her shoulder. She melted right into me.

We sat entwined for a while, only the sounds of her sniffles filled the room. I hated myself for how uncountable I felt there, with her crying. It wasn't that I didn't care about her or the situation. But grieving had been a solo experience for me. This was out of my comfort zone. How do you properly talk to someone who has lost so much? I'd been self-medicating with cheap wine and curling into a ball on the couch staring into space for hours. I wasn't exactly an expert on grief counseling.

When she pulled away, she said, "Our friendship deserved being able to hold space for the pain. That's all I ever wanted. You've been avoiding me for months. To some extent I get it. You are hurting too. It is probably taking every ounce of you to sit here with me now and keep it together—I get that. But you are the only one who understands what I am going through. So, while I understand, that doesn't mean your absence didn't hurt like hell."

My instinct was to disagree with her. Sure, the three of us had grown up together, done practically everything as a trio. But she sure as hell didn't understand what I was experiencing. Talia didn't have to wake up in a complete state of confusion and look over to see her best friend dead, sprawled out on the hard black highway. She didn't have to see her blood everywhere, a red river down the road. The sheer panic of your body being overtaken by emotions, freezing you and shaking you at the same time. It was nothing anyone could understand.

She got a phone call, a simple clean phone call letting her know Aubrey passed. I had to be there when it happened, having her blood splattered on my face and clothing. Calling to her, begging her to respond to me and being met with dead silence.

Of all the retorts that came to my mind, I went with, "I know." I was just too tired to argue.

Talia's grief made me uncomfortable. I had been wallowing in my own sadness for so long but now it was like looking into a mirror.

"Tell me what happened," she said.

I cleared my throat, not because I needed to but I was trying to give myself a few seconds to decide where to start and what to include.

Then there were footsteps, that sounded like they were coming from inside the apartment.

Talia and I looked at each other. We held each other's gaze, trying to assess the other person's reaction. She looked at me questioningly but I returned the gaze with terror in my eyes.

"Did you hear that?" I asked.

She dismissed it as normal background noise that came along with living in an apartment. I wasn't so sure. No—someone was *in* my apartment.

"I'll be right back," I said excusing myself.

With my heart pounding, I walked down the hallway and peaked into each room. I flipped on the lights to the bedroom and bathroom—nothing there. I walked back to the living room to find Talia on the couch scrolling through her phone.

She was oblivious to my terror, so she suggested we look at old photos of when we were kids. I walked over to my large wooden bookcase and pulled out a few photo albums. I handed her one of the albums and she opened it in her lap. I was still on high alert and looked around as she started turning the pages. The large pink album had photos from about second to third grade.

She squealed when we found the photos of us dressed as The Powderpuff Girls for our school's Halloween Parade. Her delight was contagious. "We were so adorable!"

I reached for her hand. "All good memories, Tal. We will always have those."

She forced a smile and her kind brown eyes momentarily locked with mine. Maybe I needed this more than I knew.

We continued to flip through the book. The school talent show; one winter break where we had a combined Christmas/Hanukkah party at Talia's house; a sleepover for Aubrey's eighth birthday party.

"All good memories," she echoed sadly.

Each page held stories that we recounted, mostly through fits of giggles.

Talia flipped to the last page.

"What the fuck!" she shouted as she tossed the album to the ground.

There on the ground was a picture of Aubrey, dead. It was from the scene of the accident, blood pooled around her. It was graphic, like out of a horror movie, and it made my stomach lurch into my throat. Her left leg was bent in an unnatural position and her arm laid behind her back.

Talia turned towards me, her eyes widening in shock. "Isabella, why the fuck do you have this photo?!"

I literally had no idea where that came from. I never had a photo from that night. Why would I? "I... I don't know," I stammered.

"You don't know why you have it? It's sick."

"No, I swear to you I do not know where that photo came from."

She looked at me doubtfully. My best friend grabbed her purse and walked towards the door. I called for her and she turned to look at me before closing the door behind her, not saying a word. The way she looked at me, with such disgust, will be etched in my memory forever.

I picked the photo off the floor to examine it, racking my brain to think where this could have possibly come from and nothing came to mind. I was pretty sure no one would have access to these photos other than the police. I walked into the kitchen and tossed the photo into the trash can.

Then, full body shaking, that night all rushed back to me. I sank to the floor and curled into a ball. It was like I was in that moment again and loud sobs that seemed to come from the pit of me released like an angry dragon.

There on the floor, I cried until I fell asleep on the cold kitchen tile.

Chapter 8

The next morning, I awoke to the sound of my front door closing and I was laying on the floor confused. I spotted the photo album open next to me. Panic set in because I hadn't taken this into the kitchen with me. My eyes panned the room as my palms became sweaty. I slowly opened the lid of the trash can to find the photo I tossed on top was gone.

Turning through possibilities of how this photo came to me, still nothing made sense. Someone must have put this photo in the album. But if that was true, how did they get into my apartment? Had they come back to take it? And would they be coming back again?

I picked up the phone and quickly dialed the police. The woman who picked up the phone spoke with a tone that seemed to imply I had some nerve calling her.

"Hi, I think someone broke into my apartment."

"Okay. What happened?"

I paused trying to figure out how to explain this.

"You there?" she snapped.

I could hear her chomping on bubble gum. "Yeah, sorry. Um… I was asleep this morning and I heard someone close my front door. And something was stolen!"

"What was stolen?"

".... a photo."

"A photo? Does this photo have any monetary value? Like was it signed by someone famous?"

"No, the photo wasn't even mine. I think they came into my apartment some time before and put the photo in my album." I was becoming increasingly aware that this sounded ridiculous.

"Okay, so someone came into your apartment to drop off a photo that has zero value and then came back to take the photo again?"

"It was a photo of my friend. She died. It was from the scene where she died," I rambled.

There was silence on the other end.

Shit, why did I call this in? I sounded like a complete lunatic and a wave of heat pooled around my cheeks. I panicked and hung up the phone.

So, the police would be no help, I concluded.

Later that night, I sat on my couch with a cup of hot chamomile tea. I had set up my space to be relaxing and comfortable in hopes that it would make me feel the same. Suddenly, the lights in the room began to flicker on and off rapidly and that triggered a full-blown panic attack.

My breathing quickened and my palms became clammy. It transported me from that moment, back to college. Back to the night that I'd give anything to forget, but haunts me, lurking and waiting to seep into any moment it can.

I always tell myself it wasn't my fault. But then I think—I shouldn't have drunk so much. I shouldn't have worn that outfit that showed off all the parts that college boys whistled at, the curves that the boys talked about with each other as if your self-worth was in each mound of flesh.

But I did do those things and after several drinks I blacked out, laying in the middle of the beer-stained hallway of the fraternity house.

When I woke up, I was right where I remembered being late last night, when I was still having the time of my life. The drinks transforming me from a shy girl to one full of confidence. I recalled my wild antics of standing on a desk, flailing my arms wildly and loudly singing songs with my friends.

But now my head felt like an ax was being repeatedly cracked on my skull and my vision was slightly blurry. I recall balling up my fists, pressing them into my eyes and twisting, trying to get my vision to clear. At the time, I thought it was the worst hangover I ever had.

Embarrassed, I got up off the floor, glad no one was awake at this hour to notice and slipped out the side exit. I was thankful no one would know that I had fallen asleep in the hallway. That would have been mortifying I thought at the time.

I had zero recollection of what actually happened in that loud, crowded hallway, but a week later, one of the fraternity brothers felt guilty and told me he needed to confess something. He invited me for a cup of coffee and over two hot bitter cups, he told me everything he witnessed.

When he first started to explain, and he became choked up, I knew my life would never be the same. He started by saying, "I should have told you sooner. My sister was a survivor of sexual assault and…"

When he said those words, 'sexual assault' it became hard to focus. Despite not knowing what he was about to say, I knew he was about to break me.

He recounted the story of that night empathetically. As I lay there on the floor, completely blacked out, many of the brothers took photos of themselves touching me inappropriately. They violated me and laughed as they did it. My body was a forbidden playground, and they trampled all over it.

He said when he saw what was happening, he stepped in and stopped them.

"Thank you," I croaked out.

"I'm going to go to campus police to tell them what I saw. I hope that's okay. Is it okay?"

I paused, so he continued. "They will keep doing this to other girls if nothing happens."

I knew he was right.

"Sure, yeah," I agreed as I lowered my head trying to hide the tears that were pooling in my eyes. Once campus police got wind of this, I'd have to meet with them and I'd lose my ability to push this out of my mind as some nightmare I imagined.

I've never had a single memory come back from that night. But I know I'll never be fully okay again. I'll never trust myself. I'll never trust myself around others.

The moment I met with the school police played in my mind. A female officer, kind and gentle, sat with me and ran through what happened that night as she showed me the evidence. Confused and devastated, I cried and she comforted me as best she could.

The photos they showed me, combined with having no recollection, set me into a deep emotion I couldn't even recognize. How do you settle in your mind that the most violating, most degrading thing to happen to you isn't part of your memories at all? This moment would be like a menacing phantom, I could never see it but it was always there trying to scare me, making me anxious, and taking away any security I used to feel.

Once the memories ran full circle, I was back in my apartment. In full panic mode, I curled into a ball, hugging my arms around my knees. My body took over as it tried to self-soothe. I rocked back and forth lightly. A repetition of sounds streamed from my mouth automatically. After twenty minutes passed, and my eyes hurt from crying so hard, I was able to slowly bring my emotions down to uncoil myself from the fetal position.

While I was able to turn off the fight or flight response, I still slightly trembled. I turned on the TV just to have some background noise. It made me feel less alone and set my dark room aglow. With old reruns of Friends going, I went in and out of sleep for the next few hours, the abrupt chorus of laughter turning on and off from the laugh track jolting me awake from time to time. I only fully fell asleep around 3:00 or 4:00 am.

Chapter 9

The week went by in a blur but it was finally the day I was dreading. It was time for the joint therapy session with my mother. It was the first time I had someone accompany me and I wasn't sure I was ready to be this vulnerable in front of others. Despite my apprehension, I had made a promise to my mother so there I was.

Dr. Price sat across from us with her legs crossed. "I'd like to thank you for joining us, Mrs. Frank."

My mother quietly nodded. "Thank you for having me. It smells nice in here by-the-way."

Her voice was meek and unsure. She wore a small pearl necklace and kept reaching up for it, spinning the pearls in her fingers. My mother kept sucking in her lower lip and I could tell she was trying to hold back her emotions. *Please don't cry before we even start*, I thought to myself.

Dr. Price asked my mother to share with me what she hoped my future would look like. My mother reached for my hand and gave it a little squeeze. I squeezed back gently to let her know it was all going to be okay.

"I look at my daughter who has always been vibrant. She was always the first to tell jokes and laugh at herself.

She was a joy to be around... she still is, obviously." She fumbled her words as if she was afraid of stepping on landmines. "I'm sorry... I've never done this before."

"Say more," Dr. Price encouraged.

"I've never been to therapy before. I'm not sure how much to say. I'm worried I'll say the wrong thing. I don't want to make things worse than they already are. I'm sorry. Maybe I'll upset Isabella... or set her off."

I had no idea what my facial expression looked like but it couldn't have been pleasant.

Dr. Price began writing on her notepad with a fountain pen. I watched as her red pen swirled across the page, mesmerized by it. As she continued to write, she looked sympathetically at my mother, nodding while she spoke.

She told my mother to say whatever she felt comfortable with and that we would work out whatever issues we had between us. Then she turned to me and asked what I felt hearing my mother's words.

"It's hard to hear, for sure. But I think I understand." I wasn't sure that I really did, though. Did she think I'd be like this forever or did she recognize that I was going through the worst time of my life? Both my mind and body were rebelling against me, unable to understand how to process all the trauma. Trauma built upon trauma. I didn't think I could be any other way but this way—a bumbling mess.

As my mother spoke, her voice became background noise and my thoughts wandered. Isolated words would break through but I couldn't follow what she was saying, too engrossed in my own thoughts.

While things were good between us now, they hadn't always been that way. My mother had me when she was young and single. My father, though he knew of me, never bothered to show his face. She was bogged down with the responsibility of having a young, energetic child and was not up to the task, still being young and energetic herself. I was often left alone.

Even when she was there, she wasn't there, opting to talk on the phone with her friends rather than do anything with me. I felt lonely when I was with her. For many years, this formed who I was. It perplexed me when people wanted to spend time with me, always carrying that maternal rejection with me.

No matter how much things had improved today, I couldn't escape how those moments molded me into who I was now. To some extent, I'd always be that little forgotten girl, not fully worthy of someone's love and attention. She was always in the background silently screaming that she needed a hug.

"Isabella?" Dr. Price called to me, snapping me back from my thoughts and into this room. The room where I should be participating and engaging with my mother. My mother who was here now, trying to repair our relationship.

"Sorry... sorry. Lots on my mind. I was thinking about work," I lied. I hadn't gone back to work since Aubrey died several months ago.

My mother gave me a puzzled look.

"Are you back at work? I thought you weren't going back for another week," my mother asked.

"No, not yet. I was just thinking about getting ready to go back. It's coming up soon and I'm pretty anxious. Probably more emails waiting for me than I can read in a day!" I quipped, trying to lighten the mood.

They both smiled politely at me and I smiled back.

For the rest of the session, I mostly listened. I had been coming here weekly for about a year so I knew Dr. Price was familiar with my side of things, she could write a book on it.

Hearing my mother's experience, seeing the pain on her face and the anguish in her voice was difficult to hear.

However, it highlighted that, for all that was wrong in our relationship, she genuinely loved me.

We thanked Dr. Price and got up to leave. "Mrs. Frank, would you mind staying a bit longer so I can speak to you one on one? Just a moment or two. Many people find it beneficial to be able to express themselves directly to a therapist." My mother looked to me for approval and I gave a slight nod encouraging her to stay.

I sat in the car pretending to be busy on my phone just to see how long she stayed inside. After about fifteen minutes, I gave up and left the parking lot. I was curious about what she felt she needed to express without me there. Hopefully, Dr. Price could help her see that this was just a temporary stage in my life. She'd have her baby girl, full of life, back… someday.

Chapter 10

The white noise machine that sat outside Dr. Price's office filled the lobby. Though we don't normally do two sessions in a week, Dr. Price encouraged me to meet with her one on one after my session with my mother. I usually don't arrive early but I had a bunch of errands to run that didn't take as long as I thought they would. So, there I was sitting in the lobby, trying to pass the time by playing some mindless matching game on my phone. I felt irked because the ads kept popping up, making it impossible to play. I closed out the app and started to text Christian.

Me: **Hey Stranger! It's been a while. Hope all is good with you!**

As I waited for a reply, I looked around the room, reopening the game. She had a poster on the wall that listed 'Things to Release' and I examined it as the ad played. Each item to release was on a colorful balloon and said things like 'things out of my control' and 'self-doubt'. I read it laughing to myself. If it was that easy none of us would be here. As I read the last one, the door to Dr. Price's office opened.

A young man walked out with one hand in his pocket; the other holding a tissue. His head was hung down like a sad puppy. When he looked up, we locked eyes and his were completely bloodshot. It was clear he had been crying. A few seconds passed with us hooked into a stare. Then it clicked. When he realized who I was, his whole facial expression morphed. His anger was red hot and I felt like his stare alone could murder me instantaneously.

"What the fuck are you doing here?" the man barked at me and I jolted in response.

It was Lucas, Aubrey's long-term boyfriend when she passed. Seeing me made him absolutely feral, like a caged, mistreated animal just being let loose, ready to seek its revenge on those that harmed it.

It took seconds to recognize him. I hadn't seen him in months and he looked completely different. When Aubrey was alive, we'd spend many nights on double dates. Everyone agreed, Aubrey had the dreamiest boyfriend. And boy did he absolutely adore her! He now had a scruffy beard, his hair was longer, unkempt and his clothes looked like he had been wearing them for days. His grief added years to him, which was understandable.

"I assume I'm here for the same reason you are." I finally responded. My words were cold and biting, attempting to mask my fear. I stood up and my knees started to buckle.

He sneered at me for a moment and then darted out the door into the parking lot.

When I got into my session, I asked Dr. Price about Lucas. "I saw my friend Aubrey's boyfriend here. Is that odd, that you see us both?"

Dr. Price rejected that criticism but also added she couldn't really speak about other clients.

"So last time we spoke, Isabella, you told me that you were in a relationship... one that you were unsure of, one that may be harmful for your wellbeing."

"I didn't say that exactly."

"No, not exactly. Are you still seeing that man?"

Her voice was stern, which was out of character for her. I had a suspicion that she had been cheated on in the past.

"No, I haven't spoken to him in days. I asked him to give me space," I lied, not having the energy to go into this with her right now. Christian and I hadn't seen each other in about two weeks but we had texted occasionally.

"Good," she replied. "You need to focus on your healing and your own mental health right now. All I want is for you to be mentally healthy and happy." With that, she moved on to asking me about other aspects of life and didn't bring up Christian again.

I lowered my voice and said, "I've been having the flashbacks again."

She changed her tone of voice to match mine. "I'm so sorry to hear that. Do you want to say more?"

"It is the same as before. It mostly happens at night, loud noises or flashing lights can trigger it. When that happens, I'm thrown back to that moment. I'm scared. How much longer do I have to deal with this?"

She listened but she didn't offer advice. I wanted her to wave a wand and cure me of all the hurt that I carried.

When our fifty minutes was up, I started to walk towards my car, scrolling through Facebook as I did. I opened the door without paying attention and started to slide into the seat, when I realized Lucas was sitting in the passenger seat.

Complete terror overtook me.

He was going to kill me. I was positive of that. Some part of my brain took over and began to speak in a calm tone. If I acted like nothing was wrong, maybe I could defuse the tension.

"Hello Lucas." I say as if it was perfectly normal for him to be sitting in someone else's car!

"I heard you found the picture I left you."

"That was you? How?"

"A shitty reporter showed them to me one day when they were interviewing me for an article about the dangers of teens and drinking. Fucking wrecked me. So, during the memorial service at your house, I left them all over, hoping you'd find them as a reminder of what you did. I want you to hurt like I do. You killed my girlfriend, the person I loved more than anything. You stupid bitch!"

He pulled at his hair and tears streamed down his face. He did not bother to wipe them away. His anguish was palpable and in any other circumstance I'd comfort him. But now, I was terrified of what he would do to me. He believed that I was the reason Aubrey was gone—and he wanted me to pay for it.

As he continued to cry into his palms, I moved my hand over to my left and quickly tapped a few times on my phone to call into Dr. Price's office. I hoped that once she heard this conversation, she would come out to help.

"Lucas, why are you in my car? We are still sitting in Dr. Price's parking lot." I said robotically, trying to drop as much information as possible. "You are not allowed to be here. I don't feel comfortable with this. You are scaring me."

He lifted his head and his eyes narrowed on me. "I don't care if you are scared. Don't you think Aubrey was scared? You deserve whatever comes to you."

With my fingers splayed, I put my hands up defensively. His hatred of me ran so deep I could feel it in my bones. He started to raise his hands up to me, reaching out for my neck when the passenger car door opened. There stood Dr. Price. The contrast of her standing while we sat low in the seats, made her feel tall, looming and authoritative.

"Lucas," she said, her voice like honey. "You don't want to do this. Come out, come back into my office and talk with me."

Lucas looked up at her. He looked like a little boy who had been caught in a lie. His rage subsided like a wave being pulled back into the ocean and all that was left was the deep sadness. She extended her hand to him and he took it briefly as he got out of the car. He slammed the door behind him and then followed her back into the office. In my rearview mirror, I kept track of him until he was fully in the building.

Once he was gone, the full realization of my terror washed over me. That had been such a traumatic experience. I gripped the wheel of my car until my fingers turned white and sore. Nausea ebbed and flowed in me and I was unsure if I would throw up right there in the driver's seat. Gazing straight ahead, I opened my mouth and screamed until I had no voice left. With everything that happened, I didn't feel safe anywhere or with anyone.

With hands trembling, I dialed the local police department. "Name, location and reason for calling?" I paused. "Isabella Frank. I'm off Klockner Road. I came out of my therapist's office and someone was in my car."

"A stranger?"

"No, my friend's boyfriend."

"And he won't get out of your car?"

"No, someone asked him to get out and he did."

"… Okay," the officer on the line replied slowly. "I'm sorry did you say your name was Isabella Frank? I have records that you called yesterday. Are you playing around with us?"

I tossed the phone into the passenger seat. Though it was muffled, I could hear, "Hello? Hello? Are you there?" No, I wasn't. I couldn't handle this anymore and I felt hollow. I sat in that seat for a while just motionless, staring straight ahead, a shell of a person.

Chapter 11

December 2023

I needed to clear my head so I threw on a hoodie to step outside. I opened the door to my apartment and on my doormat was an envelope with my name in fancy script. Loud Christmas music blared from the apartment next door. *Bah humbug,* I thought.

I reached for the envelope, thinking it was going to be a sweet note from Christian or maybe a Christmas card from my overly jolly neighbors. I pulled out the contents and gasped, tossing it to the ground. I looked down the hallway to see who could have left this. Laying on the ground was a photo of Christian, black sharpie sprawled across it:

This is MY husband.

Scrambling to get back into my apartment and then locking the door behind me, I put my back to the door and slid down it. I knew I was standing at a key moment. Either this person felt like they had sent me a message and would go away. Or this could be just the start of their reign of terror. My hands trembled as I fumbled to pull my phone out of my back pocket.

"Hey Gorgeous, Long time no talk," Christian said cheerfully.

"Yeah… I need you to come over, now." I was trying to hide the terror in my voice.

"Isabella. Are you okay? Are you safe?"

"Yes, yes. Just come. Right now! Please."

"On my way."

Fifteen minutes later there was a knock at my door. Before he could even step in, before he could even ask what was wrong, I pointed to the photo laying face down on the ground.

He picked it up and his green eyes widened. Christian ran his hand through his wavy, black hair. "Shit," was all he said as he took the photo and walked across the room to sit on the couch. As he sat there, he just repeated, "Shit, shit, shit. I'm so sorry."

"How did she get my address?"

"I have no idea."

"You need to tell me what the hell is going on… and whether or not I am safe."

"Eeee-saaah," he said sweetly as he rubbed my arm. "You are safe. She's probably just playing stupid pranks to scare you away. You are the first woman I've gone on multiple dates with since we split. I think you are safe but I can stay here on the couch and work for the day if you'd like, I can sleep on the couch tonight if you'd like. Whatever you need. First priority is for you to feel safe."

I took a seat next to him on the couch so our legs were just barely touching. This was our first time seeing each other in two weeks. Part of me wanted to move closer, to ignore that this all happened. But I knew I needed to say what I was feeling, even if it hurt to say it.

"Christian, I really like you. But we've been on just a few dates and this is just too much. I'm in a place where I should be focusing on my own issues. I'm sorry but I just can't do this right now."

Christian lowered his head. I knew there was some disappointment about what I was telling him, but also overall frustration. He couldn't escape this woman, he couldn't move on, he couldn't live a normal life. She was playing puppet master with him and he had no way to cut those strings and be free.

I put my hand on his back. "I'm sorry," I whispered. "Tell your wife we are done and to leave me the hell alone."

He didn't protest or try to talk me out of it. We sat there for a long while in silence before he got up. He leaned down and kissed me on the head. "I'll miss you, Isa. I promise you'll be safe though. Be well." Then he walked out the door closing it behind him and closing any chance we had to be together.

Chapter 12

The only person that could possibly help me navigate this would be my mother. I saw her sitting on the bench at the local park, reading a book like she always did when she had free time. That was something we had in common. You could always find us reading. It was our happy place. Give us a good book with a nice view and we are set. Add in a cup of coffee and it is pure paradise.

I hoped I wasn't going to be interrupting a good part in the book. It was difficult to be pulled from your 'book world' back into the real world full of its real problems. And I was swimming in problems right now.

When I tapped her on the shoulder she jumped. I wasn't sure who was more anxious.

"Reading anything good?" I asked, sitting down on the bench next to her.

"Yes! It's a fantasy story with dragons and faeries," she said enthusiastically while showing me the cover.

"Wish I could jump right into that world!" I said honestly.

"Well, as with anything, it isn't all magic. Their world is being taken over by evil overlords, typical fantasy genre stuff." She laughed and placed her bookmark into the book. "So how are you, my Bella?"

"I've been better, mom." I forced a smile so weak it probably looked like a straight line. My mind was a jumble. I wasn't sure where to start. People walked by on the path and I felt self-conscious of them overhearing me so I lowered my voice. "So… some strange things have been happening. Maybe it's nothing but… I'm nervous."

"What's going on?"

I began to tell her about the sounds I heard, the photo of Aubrey, the door closing in my apartment. I left out the part about Christian's wife, too worried about my mother judging my choices. I expected to see deep concern on her face but instead there was something else there—doubt.

She nodded her head as she spoke so I was surprised and a little offended when she asked, "Did anyone else hear or see these things?"

"Jesus Christ, Mom!" I snapped, upset that she was implying I might be imagining things. "And yes, Talia was there that night. She heard strange noises too. Like someone was *in* my apartment. And then she saw the photo of Aubrey. I'm telling you; I am not imagining this. I'm not making it up."

"Sweetheart, I'm not trying to upset you. I was just asking. I'm sorry." She reached to embrace me and I let her. It didn't matter how old I was, a hug from mom always helped.

"Have you talked to your therapist about this? Maybe some of these things could be a trauma response. Maybe your senses are heightened."

"I just need you to believe me. Please. That's all I need. All of this is real. All of this happened to me. And I'm terrified."

She lowered her voice in an effort to calm me. "Okay, Bella. I believe. Have you called the police yet?"

"They don't take me seriously. I really need help, mom."

"Let's get this all figured out."

This was when she was in her element. As most moms do when there is a problem, she went into action mode. She pulled out her phone and started adding security items to the cart. By the end of the week, I would have a ring doorbell, an extra lock for the door and a baseball bat. Then she googled self-defense classes and had me signed up for one next week. She asked me how to share our locations with each other on the phones and I got that set up. She sure was efficient.

Taking action helped ease my nerves and I was able to take in the beauty of the park. While my world was a mess, the rest of the world was going about their day. The birds chirped. The bare branches swayed on the trees like a parent gently rocking their baby. Mothers and fathers chased their kids on the playground. Runners moved along the path swiftly. I closed my eyes and tried to absorb this moment of normalcy.

I thanked my mom and then added, "I called down to the music store. I've rented a flute."

She smiled at me and I could tell she was truly pleased by this. "That's lovely my Bella. I hope you'll invite me over to hear you play."

We hugged goodbye and I walked the short gravel path to the parking lot. My mother, book reopened, was back in her magical world.

I waved goodbye but she didn't look up.

Chapter 13

I hadn't heard from Christian in a week. He was respecting my boundaries, which I appreciated, but I still missed him. There was a void left by the dates we had and his daily texts that brought smiles to my face.

When I arrived at my home, there were several boxes waiting on my doormat. I quickly unboxed them and began to set up all the equipment. I wasn't sure how helpful having something like a doorbell camera would be but I was desperate to have some sort of safety measures in place. Currently, being in my home made my skin crawl. Every little noise set me off like a skittish animal.

In the morning, I reviewed the footage. Living in a mid-sized apartment, most of the recorded action was neighbors passing my door to get to one of the other four units on my floor. There were some food delivery drop offs and the postal worker dropping off large packages—maybe holiday gifts.

It wasn't until I got to the second to last recorded clip, that I noticed something odd. A man walked across the camera, momentarily paused at my door, noticed it and covered his face. Then he continued on.

It was odd because he wore sunglasses and a baseball cap—in the indoor hallway. He must have noticed the camera and decided not to do whatever nefarious plan he had. I couldn't place who it was and it was driving me crazy.

Later, I decided to reach out to Talia for the first time since that night she left my apartment.

Me: **Talia, I'm sorry about what happened when you came over. I'd like to explain everything. Also, I ran into Lucas recently and I need to talk to you about it. You know I love you.**

I saw the three little dots indicating she was writing. They appeared and disappeared over and over again. Clearly, she didn't know how to respond.

Finally, her response came through.

Talia: **I love you too. We should talk but the other night was really traumatic. I'd like a mediator to be there. I hope you understand.**

I was so thankful that she was willing to work this out. It was all a misunderstanding and I knew we could get past this. We agreed to meet with Dr. Price as soon as she had an opening. There was a knock at my door and the sound of it made me jump. I slowly opened it, and there was Christian.

As soon as our eyes met, he began. "I know you needed your space, and I'll go if you want but I just wanted to…" and before he could finish, I put my arms around him.

The warmth of his body provided instant comfort. We stood there like that for a long while as time stopped. My head was buried into his shoulder, inhaling the sexy smell of his cologne. He rested his chin on my head and my body suddenly relaxed. A wave of euphoria came over me and I felt like I was glowing.

Softly, he planted a kiss on the top of my head. I looked up at him and a shot of heat rushed through my body. I raised my lips towards his and he kissed me back passionately. Oh, how I had missed him.

He gently pushed me back into my apartment and kicked the door closed behind him. I threw myself onto the couch and beckoned him towards me. He was just lowering himself down when there was a knock on the door.

"What the fuck was that?" I said manically.

Christian looked at me quizzically, his eyebrows furrowing. "I believe it's just someone at your door. Are you okay?"

I asked him to get the door. There was no one there.

"It's just a package!" he called back to me. "Should I bring it in?"

I approached the door peering at the package fully aware that I was acting bizarre. I glared at it suspiciously. Then I noticed the local music studio's name on the return address. It was my new flute.

I slowly opened the box, worried it could be a ruse. But sure enough, inside lay a black box, which I opened and saw a shiny silver flute, a music stand, and music book that I had ordered from the store.

"I didn't know you played the flute."

"I haven't in years but my mom reminded me that I wasn't half bad when I was younger. I thought it be fun to get back into it. It's got to be a more relaxing way to spend my time than doom scrolling on social media."

He chuckled. "Well let's hear it!"

I wasn't exactly prepared to play for anyone. I wasn't even sure I'd remember how to play and if I did, I might not be any good all these years later. Quickly, I set everything up and took a deep breath before beginning, hoping he wouldn't need to cover his ears.

As the sound filled the air, everything locked right into place and I flowed with the song. It felt good to be playing again and I got taken away with the music. Taken to another place that only music can take you—like you're just a little bit more alive. His eyes were locked on me the entire song and he slightly swayed with the music. When I finished Christian smiled at me in a way that I wanted to be looked at my whole life. It was like he could see me for more than I saw in myself and I wondered for a brief moment if he could fall in love with me.

"You're pretty incredible, Isa. I hope you know that."

I hadn't felt that way about myself. In fact, I felt like a total failure most days. For a moment I thought, why would this handsome, successful man want to be with me? But standing there with him, I felt pretty incredible and my heart swelled with pride. If he could see value in being with me, I needed to start seeing value in myself.

Sunlight peeked through the curtain the next morning and I pulled the large pink duvet over my head to get a few more minutes of sleep. I stretched out my arms only to hit something… someone. Christian lay next to me, fully clothed.

"Good morning, Gorgeous." He leaned over and kissed me deeply, not caring that we both hadn't brushed our teeth yet. I wrapped my arms around him. This all felt so right.

Chapter 14

As promised, Tal and I were meeting with a mediator. We spoke in whispered voices in the therapist's lobby.

"Tal, can you take a look at this?" I pulled out my phone, entered my password and pulled up the recording app. Talia looked at the footage of the man walking by my screen. She scrunched up her face and replayed it a few times.

Before I could ask her who she thought it was, she blurted out in full volume, "What the hell is Lucas doing at your place? And why is he acting like that?"

I was taken aback by how quickly she identified him.

"How do you know it's Lucas?" I asked.

She looked at me like a deer caught in headlights. "We've... been hanging out," she replied sheepishly.

"Tal, he's—"

Before I could finish, Dr. Price opened her door to allow her previous clients out, what I assumed was a mother and daughter, the teenager grimacing at her mother as they left. The mother had tears in her eyes that she wiped away with her hand. *Poor thing*, I thought.

Talia and I sat side-by-side across from Dr. Price.

Dr. Price had bags around her eyes and I noticed that her cardigan was unevenly buttoned. It wasn't that she looked bad, but she was normally a vision of perfection.

"So, ladies, what do we hope to accomplish from today's session?" she chirped brightly.

We both sat in silence for a moment, then both spoke at the same time which made us both giggle. It broke the tension and I was grateful for that. I put my arm around her briefly and she smiled at me.

"We both lost a friend; our best friend and we went a long time without speaking. It's the longest we've ever gone without talking. The whole thing was just too painful to be together without Aubrey. We've just reconnected recently. I thought it would be good if we had someone who could help us navigate talking this out."

As I spoke, Dr. Price wrote furiously on her notepad. She turned towards Talia, "Tell me how you feel about Isabella. Why did it take you both so long to reconnect?"

"Well, I suppose I had some anger directed towards Isabella since she was there that night."

I was shocked she would say this. Couldn't she see that if I had done anything wrong the police would have put me in jail? But they hadn't, I was sitting here just like her.

Before I could stop myself, I blurted out, "You're seeing her boyfriend for Christ's sake!"

Immediately I regretted it but then I got my own slap in the face when Dr. Price retorted quietly, "We don't always make the best dating decisions when we are hurting. Isn't that right, Isabella?"

I felt my eyes widen and become the size of dinner plates.

We were all looking at each other with disdain. Neither of us wanted to talk first as we sat like statues staring with our mouths slightly open.

Talia was the first to speak. "I want to be angry about what you just said but the truth is; I've felt guilty this whole time. I know it's fucked up to be dating Lucas. It is! But we have this connection to a traumatic event. We've helped each other cope."

"Trauma bonding," Dr. Price added confidently, as if anyone was asking for a fucking dictionary definition. "Go on," she said.

But I cut her off. "Talia, I think Lucas is unstable. I've been having all these strange things happen at my house and I think he's behind it. I decided to go to a self-defense class tomorrow because I'm so afraid of him."

Dr. Price suggested we do it together.

I glanced over at my best friend to gauge her reaction. She looked like she was going to say no and I was working up a list of reasons in my mind that she should go.

"Yeah… okay," she said.

"So, tell me about your relationship with Lucas, Talia," Dr. Price asked.

I monitored my breathing as she spoke so I didn't snap and say something in response that I would regret. Talia looked fragile as she spoke about him, like she was a shard of glass that could shatter into a hundred pieces if pushed.

"I ran into Lucas early one morning at the park. We were both in the parking lot stretching for a run. I walked over and greeted him. We both mentioned how we had taken up running as a way to cope. He joined me on my run and our conversation was good. He was kinda awkward and goofy. He made me laugh for the first time since… Anyway, it helped to talk about the things that were plaguing both of us."

I listened, stunned. I had known none of this. Of course, how could I? I'd basically blocked Talia from my life up until recently.

She continued. "Well, we kept meeting unexpectedly at the park around the same time, until finally we made plans and it became a daily thing we did together. Same time, same place. Then we started getting breakfast after… then he started reaching for my hand during breakfast." Talia turned toward me. "It wasn't planned on either of our parts. It just happened. We found comfort in each other."

I didn't like that they were dating, for multiple reasons. It felt like she was betraying Aubrey, which I know doesn't make sense since she isn't even alive. It just felt wrong. I was also very worried for her safety because Lucas was out of his mind. Talia deserved a happy and healthy relationship.

"It looks like there is something you want to say," Dr. Price said, looking at my friend.

"Well…" She paused.

"Go on. You are in a safe space."

"When I was at Isabella's house recently, we were looking through photos. She had a photo of Aubrey, dead." Her voice became nearly inaudible and then she began deep huffing breaths.

I rubbed her back as I looked at the therapist. "I swear I didn't put that photo in the album."

"I know that now. Lucas admitted to me that he did it awhile back. I know I should have said something sooner. He's really sorry. It was meant for you... not for me." Again, her voice trailed off.

"Why bring it up then? I thought you were angry that I had this as... some sort of sick trophy."

"God no. It just... broke me. I'm shattered. It puts me closer to that place then I ever thought I'd have to be."

She reached for me and we embraced, our tears soaking the other's shoulder. I whispered into her ear that I was so sorry that she had to see that. "I love you," I whispered over and over. I could feel her head nodding, acknowledging me but not returning the words.

As our session was wrapping up, Talia looked at Dr. Price, though her comment was for me. "I've been thinking about this for a few days after what happened and I think it would be helpful if we went to the crash site together. Like a small memorial service, just for the two of us."

I didn't want to do this, not right now. I waited for Dr. Price to respond but she just glared at me, awaiting my response. I looked at Talia and she was chewing on her lower lip. Water started pooling in the corner of her eyes. We continued to look at each other for a while and I realized she wouldn't respond.

"I think that is a lovely idea," I said as I forced a pathetic smile.

We left the session with some progress made on the situation but also seemed to have added a whole lot more that we needed to work out. What a complicated mess of an hour I thought to myself.

In my head, I'd thought we'd walk in and in the space of an hour resolve this major trauma that had rocked both of our worlds.

I felt stupid for being so naïve.

Chapter 15

The next night I met Talia in the parking lot of the martial arts studio. They were having a series of self-defense classes specifically for women. As we sat in the waiting area, I looked around at the other ladies. I wondered what brought them there—a former close call that made them want to be prepared next time? An obsession with true crime that warped their mind into always expecting danger around every corner? Or were they currently in real danger? I said a little prayer that they were all safe and just taking precautions.

A short, stocky man in all black walked into the waiting area. He looked like the type of guy who would hit on every woman at a party and have that 'any woman would do' attitude. His vibes were off and I immediately disliked him.

"Ready?" he said with that over-the-top enthusiasm all trainers seem to have.

Must be from all the endorphins from working out so often. I couldn't have met his level of enthusiasm if I tried. Talia and I followed the trainer and the other women into the studio.

"Good evening, ladies. My name is Chad." Of course it was. Chad puffed out his chest as he spoke. "The world is filled with bad guys who have bad intentions. Not me of course!" he said, and was met with some uncomfortable laughter. "Over the next few sessions, I will teach you ladies how to protect yourselves from the dangers that are all around you. Think you are safe doing a late-night grocery run? Think again! Going for an early morning jog? Think again! If you watch the nightly news, you know that women have been attacked just going about their daily lives. You must always be vigilant and prepared to defend yourself. So, let's get started keeping you ladies safe." He flashed a big toothy smile.

Chad asked for a volunteer. I didn't raise my hand but a very petite blonde woman sitting near me did. He selected her, I suspect because she was one of the few women here who wasn't taller than him.

As he began to demonstrate the first move, the woman followed his directions and was able to easily escape his grasp. I wondered if we would be able to recreate this if we were in a real physical altercation. The scenario played in my mind which caused my heart rate to accelerate. It suddenly felt too warm in here. Too stuffy, too small. Too much of everything.

Then Chad asked for another volunteer and no one raised their hand.

"Okay this pretty lady," he said pointing to me. I tried to refuse but he wouldn't let me. "There is no 'opting out' if someone is set on doing you harm."

He explained to the group that he was going to try to grab me from behind and flip me to the ground. He then reviewed what I should do to break away. His thick arms wrapped around my waist and he grabbed hard.

Feeling uncomfortable, I didn't do what he said to resist and was laid out flat on the ground. I could hear and see him, but my brain wouldn't process any of it. My breath became shallow. As dizziness overtook me, the world around me went fuzzy. The fact that I even had to be here, was pulling me down into that black hole. I quickly got up and walked out of the studio and into the bathroom, overcome with both embarrassment and fear.

In the bathroom, I went into a stall, not caring or even checking how clean or dirty it was and sank to the cold tile floor. I sat there a long while, not even sure how long. It sounded like someone called after me, but I couldn't be sure. My brain was buzzing and couldn't process much. Then a soft knock came at the stall door.

I didn't answer.

"Isabella?" I could see Talia's bright pink sneakers outside the door. "Are you... sick? Everything okay?" she pressed again trying to get a response. I centered myself and forced myself to push through the total lack of energy. "Yeah, sorry. Just had a headache and needed a second of quiet." She sank down onto the floor, the door to the stall separating us. Through the large gap at the bottom, she slid her hand through to my side. We sat there, holding hands silently for a few minutes as I focused on steadying my breath. Finally, I emerged from the stall and walked out with her.

I spent the next half of the class robotically doing the movements, each movement wiping out all the energy I had. When Chad came around and placed his hands on me to self-correct certain positions, I would cringe. All I could hope was that I'd retain something from this class in case I needed it.

Something inside me told me I would.

Talia walked me to my car. She knew something was wrong but I hadn't told her about my mental health struggles.

"Was that triggering?" she asked.

"Mmm hmm," was all I could muster.

"We don't have to do it again if you don't want to," she said.

"Yeah, maybe this isn't the place for me. I think I'll search for a less cringy instructor."

"Come on! You didn't love the pint-sized prince?"

I chuckled and we hugged goodbye. The class played in my mind as I drove home. I was eager to go straight to bed.

Chapter 16

This time of year was always so beautiful in my neighborhood. Each person decorated their balcony for the holidays. The twinkling lights warmed these chilly winter New Jersey nights.

My neighbor Ms. Vines sat on the bench outside, all bundled up. It didn't matter the time of year, you could always find her sitting on the bench around this time of day.

"Hello, dear," she said cheerily. "Your boyfriend was by, sweet boy, he left something on your door."

I was intrigued so after making a bit of small talk, I bounded up the stairs taking two at a time. It had been ages since someone had given me flowers and I was hoping to find a fresh bouquet on my doorstep. I wondered if Christian knew my favorite flower, which was daffodils.

When I got to my floor, I could see down the hall that there was nothing on the mat. Dreams of flowers were replaced with disappointment. I approached my door and that's when I saw a printed paper taped to it. On the paper, in huge font, read '**BEWARE OF HER**'.

I pulled down the paper, crumpled it up and tossed it into the trash.

Quickly, I reviewed my doorbell app to see who left it here. But there was nothing for the entire day. Someone must have disabled it, which I didn't even know was possible. My main security protection was gone and now this person wasn't just trying to scare me—they were trying to make my neighbors think that I was dangerous. I couldn't figure out their angle or their end game.

With so much adrenaline running through my veins, sleep wasn't an option for me. I sat on my couch, with the baseball bat by my side. Soft music played from my phone, in a fruitless effort to calm my nerves. Each time I heard a noise, which were just sounds of my neighbors in their own apartments, I'd place my hand on the bat. I'd grip it hard until my fingers became tense.

I pulled out the most recent book I borrowed from the library. It was a story about two college lovers who lost touch, married other people, divorced and then reconnected in Paris. If I had to be up all night, at least I could try to get into a good story. I attempted to take myself into the plot, straight to the bustling streets of Paris but my mind was distracted. Every sentence I read needed to be reread several times in order to comprehend it. This was pointless.

Thud! Went the book as I slammed the hardcover shut in frustration.

I needed to feel proactive about the situation. At first, I tried watching videos on YouTube about self-defense.

That didn't help.

Flipping through Instagram to pass the time, an adorable video of a Golden Retriever puppy running into a kiddie pool popped up. A new, exciting idea popped in my head. Getting a dog who could offer some level of protection was what came to mind first. After several hours, I had all the information I needed on what breeds I wanted and what local shelters had the types of dogs that would meet my needs.

As the sun began to creep up over the horizon, I convinced myself it was safe to fall asleep. Hunger caused my stomach to cramp but my focus was on my more immediate need of sleep. I quickly fell asleep right on the couch in the clothes I had been wearing yesterday, too tired to even make it to bed.

When I woke up, there was about an hour until the local shelter closed. I rushed over, hoping the dogs posted online were up to date. When I arrived, a plump woman name Karen greeted me. I told her about my situation and how I'd like to see about adopting a guard dog for my apartment. She offered me a seat at the table in the entrance.

"I understand you'd like protection and we can find a dog that meets those needs but a dog primarily known for protection may not be best for an apartment. They are mostly larger dogs, who would need a lot more space to run around and play."

This was a stranger sitting in front of me but I decided to expose a bit of my story. "I really feel like I need a dog that can provide some level of protection. I've been having someone leave threatening messages at my house and I suspect they may have even broken into my apartment." Tears began welling in my eyes. The stress of this situation was pulling me open at the seams. "Please help me, I really, really need something," I pleaded.

Karen was incredibly sympathetic to my situation. She put her hand on my shoulder and said, "Let's go back and look at the pups. We can talk about the pros and cons of each in regards to you feeling safe, as well as what would be a good fit for apartment living. Remember—this is going to be a member of your family so you want to make sure that they are comfortable in your space."

Each dog was in a large walled-off area, with plenty of toys, food and water. The pens were clean. It was clear that these dogs were well taken care of while they lived here awaiting their forever owner.

As we walked, my throat started to tighten and I wasn't sure what was causing me to choke up. Was it sadness from these dogs being without a family, was it the joy of getting a new dog... or maybe just overall instability causing emotions to ebb and flow on a whim?

I was originally hoping to get a German Shepard or a Rottweiler but was open to whatever Karen suggested. After showing me several dogs, Karen said, "And this is Winston. He's a four-year-old Shih Tzu."

Right away I knew this was my dog. Sure, he wasn't going to save me from any scuffles but he'd alert me if there was an issue. He'd also provided some much-needed companionship. A dog, this dog was just what I needed.

I filled out the paperwork and hoped to hear back soon if I was approved.

As we had agreed, Talia and I met at the site where Aubrey lost her life, and where I had one of the most traumatic nights of my life. I pulled up to the spot with Christian in the passenger seat for support. She was already there, waiting patiently. She got out of her car, flowers in hand, tears already streaming down her face. I began to cry also and the heat stung my face. I simultaneously knew I needed to be here and wanted to run away and never think of this spot again.

"I'll hang back so you two can say what you need to say. But I'm here if you need me." He kissed my cheek and I walked over to my long-time friend.

Talia carried the bouquet of flowers to the site and took crumpled lined paper from her pocket. She began to read, pausing often to allow herself to calm down enough to continue. "Aubrey, each day without you, feels like a day I shouldn't have either. It is hard to exist without you, knowing I can't call you to hear your triumphs; and you would have had so many. I was very angry that you were gone and I blamed everyone."

I look over at her at this remark but she isn't looking at me. I moved closer to her, seeing if she wanted to be embraced.

She continued, "But the truth is, life isn't always fair and sometimes really terrible things happen to really, really, good people. And you were the best of people, Aubrey."

When she stopped speaking, she took a few steps forward and laid down the flowers she'd brought; a handful of wildflowers, bursting with color. I was so captivated by her speech that I had drowned out the sounds of cars passing, only now realizing how busy it was. I walked to where she stood and laid down a small stuffed animal, a panda. Aubrey always loved pandas.

Talia turned to me and opened her mouth to speak but I cut her off. "That was…" My voice cracks but I pushed through it. "Talia, that was so beautiful. That healed my heart."

She put her arm around my back as we looked at the flowers and panda on the ground. "I feel better too. I know this was hard for you, to be here. Thank you for doing this for me. For Aubrey."

We both walked over to Christian where I introduced the two for the first time. Seeing as we were by the side of the highway, it was a quick meeting but I hoped they got a good first impression of each other. When Talia leaned in to hug me, she whispered in my ear, "He's a keeper!"

Chapter 17

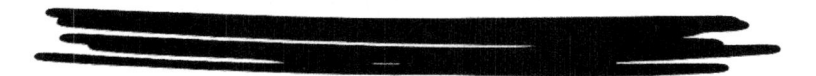

January 2024

My application had been accepted and several weeks later, Winston had settled into his new home. We had a flow to our day together and I was enjoying the stability that those routines gave me. Around 6:30 am each morning, Winston would softly cry from the foot of my bed and I'd crawl out from under the covers and take him for a one-mile walk. After giving him food and water, I'd get ready for the day.

Whenever I returned home, he'd barrel towards me and I'd duck down to be at his level as he covered me in kisses. I'd take him out for another mile walk before even meeting my own needs. We'd spend the rest of the evenings cuddled on the couch until we both jumped into my bed. Just to do it all over again the next day. The comfort he brought me was indescribable and he had no idea how much he meant to me.

The weather was unseasonably warm for a January afternoon so I grabbed his purple leash and we set off to the local dog park. He was living his best life in that park. After twenty minutes of fetch, I sat down on the wooden bench and scrolled through my phone as Winston pranced around the grass field.

I lifted my head when he started to happily yap. Crouching down at the gate, petting my dog was Lucas. The shock of seeing him made me momentarily freeze. "Jesus Christ... why are you here?" I demanded.

He looked up at me briefly but didn't respond. He went back to petting the dog as if I wasn't there.

Something overtook me, like a motherly instinct and I felt brave and bold. Surprised by my own assertiveness, I shouted, "Are you stalking me?!"

Again, he just continued to pet Winston and I became nervous he was here to hurt him. I dashed over and quickly scooped Winston up into my arms. "Get the hell away from my dog and get the hell away from me. Come around one more time and I'll call the cops."

He looked up at me with dead eyes. He looked awful, nothing like the handsome man my best friend had loved so much. I almost felt sorry for him.

"The cops won't be able to help you," he said in a low voice.

I swore in my head and knew he was right. Lucas had become absolutely terrifying and I had no idea how to protect myself from him. I quickly left the dog park with

Winston in tow, often checking behind me but I could no longer see him.

Sitting on my couch, I felt too paranoid to be in my own home. I had to go somewhere that Lucas couldn't find me. I pulled out my phone and texted Christian.

I typed: **I've met another man and he's stolen my heart.**

I pressed send and then sent a photo of Winston.

He quickly responded.

Christian: **He's adorable. Can I swing by in an hour after work to meet him?**

Me: **I'd rather come to your place. Is that okay?**

I waited for the three little dots. They kept appearing and disappearing. The fact that he told me he was married nagged in the back of my head. Maybe I'd never be invited over. Chirp!

Christian: **Yes, absolutely but it's a mess so can you give me an extra hour? I'd hate for you to find out I'm a total slob so early in the relationship.** And then he sent the laughing/crying emoji.

I snuck a toothbrush, deodorant, and a change of socks and underwear into a large purse just in case he asked me to stay over. My goal was to be prepared but not presumptuous. Winston's bag of supplies was larger than mine as I packed his food dishes, kibble, toys, bed and leash.

Walking into Christian's home for the first time, I thought it was very stylish. The home was decorated in muted tones that gave it a warm and welcoming feel. The place felt more like the home of a successful couple than a bachelor. I let Winston off the leash. Christian got on his knees and Winston jumped right into his lap.

"I guess he likes you!"

Christian laughed and mused, "Yeah, I'm a pretty likable guy."

After lots of pets and licks, he stood up and kissed my lips. Winston went off to explore more and I wished he could report back to me on his findings. We embraced for a long while.

When he loosened from me, he said, "Welcome to my home, Isa. Would you like some wine?" We walked into the kitchen and he had quite the collection of wine bottles.

"Sure, do you have white?"

"I have everything," he laughed. "They aren't anything fancy, but I do like having different types of wines to go with dinners."

He was being modest; I recognized some of the labels. Labels I passed in the liquor store because the price tag was too high for my income. He selected a bottle and showed it to me. I approved.

"I'm alone most nights so I rarely open them. I'm glad you are here."

As he poured my glass he said, "I don't mean to pry, but you seem a bit nervous. Everything okay?"

Shit, had it been that noticeable? I thought getting away from my home, from Lucas would calm me down. I decided it was time to tell him what was really happening.

We settled down in his living room. Christian sat close to me so our legs touched. He handed me the wine glass and tipped his towards mine causing a light clinking sound. My heart rate started to accelerate as the thoughts of everything that happened stormed around in my head.

"Back in high school, probably our sophomore year, Aubrey started dating a guy named Lucas. We'd often hang out as a group—Aubrey, Lucas, Talia and I. Talia and I dated people but never anything as serious as Lucas and Aubrey. They were like the 'It' couple of our high school. Even though they were young, they were very much in love and I liked him a lot at the time. He was good to her and he was fun to have hang out with us. That's why what I'm about to say is so confusing to me. I just never thought he had this in him."

Christian looked at me and cocked his head to the side, his eyebrows furrowing.

"I don't have solid proof, well not anything the cops would accept, but he's been harassing me and I'm starting to think he might be following me. I think he's been leaving me messages at my home—in my home. I think he's been inside while I was there—"

"Wait what?" Christian's voice was a mix of concern and astonishment. "Isa, you have to tell the cops."

I shook my head, the fruitlessness of the last two phone calls to the police making me cringe. "Believe me, I've tried. It is pointless. Let me have Talia talk to him. They are dating now."

Christian grimaced.

Yeah, I thought, I had the same reaction. He pleaded with me to at least try one more time with the police and I promised I would try to reach out again.

Winston hopped up onto the couch and nestled between us. We laughed and it took us out of the seriousness of the moment. Thank God for that. I didn't want to think about Lucas or all the trouble he'd been causing me lately.

Christian put down his wine glass onto the marble coffee table. He turned toward me and said, "You don't have to say yes but I'd love it if you could come to my friend's party this weekend. It's like a belated holiday party. They all have kids so doing it after Christmas just made sense for them. But it will still be festive and boozy. I know you are more introverted so if you wanted to only stay for a bit that would be fine too."

My cheeks flushed red. He was right, I loved the idea of parties but as soon as I arrived, I was overwhelmed and couldn't make small talk for the life of me. I worked much better in small groups but for the opportunity to be more involved in his life, I'd take that chance.

"Yes, I'd love that," I said beaming at him. He kissed my cheek gently. I cupped his chin in my hand and went in to kiss his lips. Christian stood up and extended a hand to me. He guided me to his room where I spent the night. I was falling hard for this man.

Chapter 18

The next morning, I woke up to my back being rubbed. I turned toward him. "So... does this make me your girlfriend?" I asked.

"Do we need labels?" Ouch! This wasn't the response I was expecting and I pulled back.

"Are you seeing anyone else?"

He shook his head. "You know I'm technically still married. I just think things are complicated right now. I enjoy being with you though."

"You enjoy being with me?" I practically shouted. "For fuck's sake Christian you slept with me last night! But you can't be serious with me? That's such bullshit."

He sighed. I could tell he was weary and I started to back down. The stress of the never-ending divorce was weighing on him.

"I know this situation is shitty, but I spoke with my lawyer last night and everything should be settled in two weeks. And as soon as it's official, I'll make you my girlfriend, properly. I care about you a lot and I want to start this on the right foot. Okay, Isa?"

I narrowed my eyes at him. "Fine."

I rolled out of bed and grabbed Winston's leash. He wagged his tail and then started to circle around himself. My face broke into a huge smile. Dogs were always so happy, just the act of going out for a few minutes to relieve himself made him overjoyed. Why did humans have to be so complicated?

I opened the front door and right away was lurched forward onto the front lawn. Winston bolted toward the tree at the edge of Christian's front yard. I stood and looked around as he did his business. I noticed a red car parked across the street, someone sitting in it with a magazine wide open covering most of their face. It was a comically immature disguise.

"Come boy!" But of course, Winston wasn't trained yet and he had no desire to come back in. I quickly pulled on the leash and tried to walk toward the house but he wouldn't budge, like a stone statue.

"Now!" I said as if he would understand, and I scooped him up and bolted for the door. I fumbled with the door handle. Shit, I had locked myself out. With an open palm, I began to pound on the door. Christian opened the door and I pushed past him into the house.

Breathlessly I panted, "Lucas. Lucas followed me here. He's sitting outside in the red car." Christian cracked the door and peered outside.

"Where?"

I went to the large bay window and pointed at the car.

Christian looked in the direction I was pointing. "That's my neighbor. He sometimes sits in his car to read because, as he likes to tell anyone that would listen, 'his kids are loud little demon hell raisers'."

"Oh." I laughed out of embarrassment but Christian didn't smile.

"Are you okay, Isa?" He took my chin in his hand to move my gaze to meet his.

"I'm fine. It was just a silly misunderstanding."

Again, he stressed that if I was really that worried, I needed to contact the police and again, I insisted I'd talk to Talia first.

A new dog is a great way to get a conversation going. When I told Talia, I had just gotten a dog that I'd love her to meet, she was at my house in twenty minutes. Winston jumped into her lap and after the obligatory licking, he settled next to her as she stroked his tan and white fur. This lulled him to sleep and he began softly snoring as he lay beside her.

I could tell she was feeling relaxed, a sweet dog will have that effect on people. I hoped that would help with the difficult conversation we were about to have. "How are things going with Lucas?"

She gazed down at the dog, focusing on petting his head softly. Talia paused for a while before responding. She pulled at the sleeves of her oversized blush pink sweater to cover her hands. "It's hard to say. We are both so fucked up. And then we decided to get into a fucked up relationship."

I blew out a long breath. "You know I love you and you know I would always support you." She nodded slightly. "I'm worried Lucas isn't right for you. I've told you this before but it needs repeating—I think he's dangerous."

She moved back from me and shook her head rapidly.

"Someone has been coming to my home, leaving messages on my door. He followed me to the dog park. I even think he entered my house. He's dangerous and I need you to be careful."

I asked her if she had noticed any strange behavior. She looked at me with pleading eyes before responding, "One day, when we got into his car, he plugged his phone into the car and the GPS started up. It had your address as the last place. I'm sorry, Isabella. I had no idea. He's become increasingly erratic and secretive. Always hiding his phone…" her voice trailed off, a small tear dropping down her face and onto Winston's head. "But he has a good heart- it's just broken."

I put my hand on her shoulder to offer her comfort. She began to pet his head again and he licked her hand, unaware of the serious conversation we were having. I asked her to stay away from Lucas and she was noncommittal. Looking at her demeanor though, I felt something wasn't right. "Is there something else?"

Now she was fully crying, bringing her hands to her face. "Listen, I didn't say anything because I didn't know how to interpret it. Don't hate me, okay? A night or two ago Lucas stayed the night. One thing led to another and we were… intimate, for the first time." Her words came out cautiously and she eyed me for a reaction to gauge how to proceed.

I wasn't sure what was coming next but I gave her a nod to encourage her. Sure, I might not like what I am about to hear, but I still needed to hear it. My life may depend on it.

"He somehow felt both angry and detached at the same time during it, too rough, too cold for me."

"Did he hurt you?" I interjected a little too loudly.

"No… well not physically. After we were together, he cried. Uncontrollably. I should have felt bad for him—but I felt mortified for myself. I hated him in that moment. He fell asleep on my bed and I never said a word to him. I sat on the chair in the corner and just glared at him." She ran her fingers through her hair as she took a pause in her story.

"And then?" I coaxed.

She sucked in her lower lip and then went on. "He must have had a nightmare. In his sleep he kept yelling, 'No!' He shouted no over and over again. Then he said your name. Why would he say your name?" I shrugged my shoulders and she continued. "I walked over and shook him hard. When he opened his eyes, I didn't mention what he'd said. It was like 2:00 am and I didn't care. I was still so angry that he ruined our first time together. Probably our last time too. I just told him he should go home. And he did without even objecting." She swallowed deeply and then lowered her head unable to look at me.

"I'm sorry, Tal," I said, trying to comfort my friend but the fear that Lucas was definitely out to get me overtook my thoughts. Why had he said my name? My hand trembled as I reached to pet Winston, who had been in her lap this whole time. My touch made him stand up and come to me. I petted his head, so grateful that he had come into my life. I needed his comfort more than ever.

Chapter 19

I hadn't been back to work since before Aubrey passed. It was my first day at the office and the jitters were so strong I felt ill. In my closet, all I saw were old, ugly clothes. Nothing felt right for the first day back. I pushed hangers back and forth, unimpressed.

Finally, I settled on a tweed mini skirt, a tight black sweater and tan knee-high boots. I loosely curled my hair and then ran my fingers through it so it had a beach wave look. Lastly, I applied some natural makeup. My reflection in the mirror looked ready. I added a ring, a friendship ring that Aubrey had given me several years ago. The bright red stone popped against my neutral outfit. I was ready... or at least I looked the part.

The office chatter was strong as I approached. I had been working in this non-profit for two years now and I enjoyed it here. The work we did made me proud; we helped families experiencing domestic violence to find safe living spaces. We made house visits to support partners and their children. We had links to local resources such as therapy that could assist families. Overall, it was a good organization that helped the community.

As I opened the door, the bell chimed and people turned towards me. The chatter immediately stopped and my confidence drained away from me. While I just wanted to run out and not come back, I forced myself to go to my desk.

I sat in my comfortable swivel chair, turned on my computer and pretended like everything was fine. All I wanted to feel was normal again. That's why I was back here after all these months. I had hundreds of emails to sift through so at least that could keep me busy for a few hours. While I focused on my inbox, I could ignore the hushed tones around me.

My boss's familiar heels clinking got louder and louder as she approached my desk. She propped an elbow on the cubicle wall.

"Welcome back," she said in a flat tone. No one was sure how to act around me.

"It's good to be back, Diane. How have you been?"

"Fine. But more importantly, how have you been, Isabella?"

"I'm great!" The forced enthusiasm in my voice sounded stupid and awkward and I immediately regretted it. "Well, I'm getting by," I tried to self-correct.

She looked at me for a few extra seconds before responding, "I'm glad to see you back. Let us know if you need anything."

I reassured her I was fine and turned back to my many, many waiting emails. Delete, delete, spam, generic response, delete.

And then an email caught my eye. It was from earlier today. The email had been sent from an email account I didn't recognize but the subject line is what got my attention. 'Help now' it read. I opened the email.

> *Hi, I'm not sure if this is the right organization to contact, but I'm really concerned and I don't know where to go. My son hasn't hurt me or anyone but I'm afraid he will. He's been withdrawn and quick to anger. He's never been like this before. He's been hiding things from me and everything I say to him makes him lash out at me. Just with words... for now. I guess I'm reaching out because I thought maybe someone here would have some advice on how I can help my son.*

I just starred at the screen for a long while. In the past, I would have been quick to respond but having been gone so long I wasn't sure what to say. After a few minutes of absorbing the message, I walked over to my co-worker Troy's desk. He was playing Candy Crush on his phone when I tapped his shoulder.

He jumped a mile high as he turned around. "Oh phew, it's just you."

"I love being greeted like that," I joked. I told Troy about the email and asked him to take the case, explaining that I didn't know if I was ready to take on a case just yet.

"So, you just got back and you're already offloading work onto other people?" He tried to hide his mouth flipping into a smile.

I playfully pushed on his shoulder but I really did appreciate that he was treating me normally. Not like everyone else in the office who felt like I was a landmine they needed to avoid. Like stepping near me might set off an explosion. Troy promised to reach out to the mother and would confirm with me once he had made contact.

The last hour of work dragged on so slowly. I rapidly tapped my pencil on my desk. The loud rapping sound echoing in the small cubicle. I began to adjust the photos on the wall just to pass the time. Photos of a life that no longer existed. Aubrey, Talia and I at our middle school dance. Aubrey, Talia and I at the Belmar beach from last summer, matching swimsuits and pink smoothies in our hands. And countless photos of the three of us just hanging out, being silly. My mind drifted to some of those memories when a hand touched my shoulder and I yelled. Loudly.

I whipped around and Troy was standing there, shocked. "It's just me! Are you okay?"

"No, not really, but is anyone actually okay?" That was rather embarrassing.

He pulled up a rolling chair from the empty cubicle next to me. I always liked Troy as a co-worker. He had one of those remarkable people skills where he listened to you speak with such focus that you felt like you were the only person in the world. You felt special when you were having a conversation with him.

"I spoke to the mother that emailed you, Ms. Santiago. She seemed in a rush to get off the phone. When I asked if her son was listening in or nearby she said no. So, I tried to ask her questions about the situation and she was just trying to end the conversation as quickly as possible. I told her I couldn't really help her or give her advice if she didn't give me details about the situation. Then she abruptly hung up. I tried calling back twice but she didn't pick up. I'm going to go out for a visit tomorrow just to make sure she's okay."

Troy was a good guy and very good at his job. He had a very calming demeanor that got people to open up—even about difficult situations. I was surprised he hadn't made any progress with Ms. Santiago but I thanked him for trying. "Keep me posted about the visit," I said.

Three more minutes until I could clock out. Two more. One. I bolted up, grabbed my purse and coat. Then I swiftly made my way to the door. My first day back was exhausting and I just wanted to go home, cuddle with Winston and go to sleep. I put the keys in the ignition and then just sat there. The energy to even drive home was gone. Unsure if I could make it the twenty minute drive, I closed my eyes and fell asleep.

There was a rapping on my window and I shot up straight in the driver's seat. I turned my head to the sound, and there was Troy.

"Are you okay?!" he shouted through the door.

I cracked open the car door. "Shit Troy. How many times are you going to make me jump out of my seat today?"

"My goal was four so I've got two more before day's end." He smiled.

I laughed. "Sorry, I was just tired and wanted to get a quick cat nap before driving home."

"It's 7:00 pm. You've been here for two hours? Are you sure you're okay? Like sure, sure. Because if not, I can give you a lift."

I assured him I was fine. Feeling a bit silly, I turned the key and the car's hum started.

By the time I got home, it was nearly 7:30. I should be starving but my appetite was non-existent. After walking Winston, we cuddled on the couch, pulling the large blue blanket over me. I turned on a TV show that I knew I would only use as background noise. The soft light it would spread around the room was an extra bonus. Very quickly, I fell back asleep until my alarm clock for work went off.

I considered calling out of work although calling out on my second day back wouldn't be a good look. I even started to put in the phone number but then deleted it. It was time to get my life back to normal. Plus, all my savings had dried up so I really needed the paycheck. This, I told myself, would be part of the healing process. Going out with friends, getting back to work, dating, finding joy in hobbies—all those needed to resume for my own mental health.

When I walked into the office for my second day, people seemed a little more relaxed to be around me. I suppose the fact that I didn't freak out or cry yesterday led people to believe I was basically okay now. Being back here did force me to fill my days with more than sleeping and the occasional binge eating.

I spotted Troy's cubicle was empty and assumed he might have called out sick. Just before lunch he returned and made a beeline for my cubicle. Curiosity got the best of me so I skipped greetings and just blurted out, "What?!"

"First, rude. Second, good morning, Isabella. Third, I thought it would be a good idea if you shadowed me for my visit to Ms. Santiago. It would help you ease back into it."

I tilted my head to silently say, 'I'm considering it.'

"Come on, I'll drive." I followed, excited to escape the monotony of the office.

We went to her house and Troy rang the bell while I stood back on the step below. Ms. Santiago appeared at the door and opened it just a crack and she peered through the small opening looking very uncomfortable. I could see the silhouette of her son behind her, the one she emailed about.

"Hi, Ms. Santiago. I'm Troy—"

"Please go away," her voice croaked.

I let out a big puff of air. I didn't like how this was going.

"Could we please come in and speak with you?"

"No, I don't think so."

Troy looked back at me so I approached the door. "Ma'am, do you have any questions for us? Any ways you'd like assistance?"

She started to say that she had to go but then her son moved closer behind her as he said, "Who is there?"

She was fidgety and her eyes were darting back between Troy and I and back at her son. Clearly, we shouldn't leave this situation—this woman was in real fear.

The young man now stood side-by-side with his mother. There standing before me was Lucas Marino. My jaw opened slightly from the shock and I stared at Troy waiting for him to react. But he had no idea about Lucas and his relentless harassment.

I excused myself, telling Troy I wasn't feeling well. Being fully aware of why I hadn't been into work for so long, he didn't think anything of it. He didn't seem to notice the terror in my eyes at seeing Lucas. I sat in the car until he returned.

"I know you are getting asked this question far too often but, are you okay?" he asked when he slid into the driver's seat a few minutes later.

"Um, that guy—we know each other from high school. What happened after I left?" I tried to keep my voice casual. The fact that I worked for an organization that helped protect women from toxic relationships and was hiding my own issues was hard to reconcile.

"Isabella, there has to be more to it than that. You aren't telling me something. The last thing he said to me was 'Tell her to be careful'."

"What the hell does he mean by that, Troy?"

"It means ask for help if you need it—before it is too late. It means you need to watch your back."

Chapter 20

This would be my first time meeting Christian's friends and I hoped to make a good impression, which hasn't always been the case. Hell, I don't think I've ever made a good impression on my date's friends. My shyness and to be honest my insecurities make me so unsure of myself around new people that I become extremely quiet. I have things I want to say, ideas that pop in my head, but they never come out of my mouth. So, every single time, I get the report back, 'My friends thought you didn't like them'.

I was hoping a little bubbly would help me overcome that.

The first step was to do my hair and makeup. It was an evening event at someone's home so I kept it simple but definitely more than I would do for our regular dates. I slipped into a little sparkly red dress that I ordered online. Luckily, it fit like a glove. Faux diamond earrings and a tennis bracelet completed the outfit. Lastly, I slipped into two-inch strappy heels. It was the perfect look for a (belated) holiday party.

My doorbell rang, and there stood Christian in jeans and an ugly Christmas sweater. "Oh." Fell from my mouth.

"You look incredible!" he gushed as he looked me up and down.

"Thanks, but you didn't tell me it was an ugly sweater party. Am I overdressed?"

"Overdressed? No. Overthinking it? Yes." He pulled me close to him and whispered in my ear, "You look so hot."

My cheeks blushed to the shade of my dress. Hand in hand we headed to the party.

When I got there, sure enough, everyone was in an ugly Christmas sweater. The feeling of being out of place rattled inside of me. I snapped right into being too shy to talk.

Christian began introducing me to his friends and I smiled politely and greeted them back and then… nothing. It was as if I had a hand pressed over my mouth forbidding me to speak.

He sensed my unease and tried to pull me into conversations.

"Isabella is a musician."

"Oh yeah? What do you play?" asked a guy whose name I had already forgotten.

"Flute."

"Cool… cool."

"Excuse me, I'm just going to grab a drink," I said, making a beeline for the table with champagne flutes pre-poured. I grabbed one and downed it. Then another. I knew two would get me to that sweet spot of being slightly buzzed. Just enough to get me chatty.

Two women walked by and grabbed a drink. "I like your dress," she said to me. I was unsure if she was serious or mocking me for being so out of place. They started to walk away, chatting, not lowering their voices at all. "She looks like a big red flag." They laughed and the other one quipped, "Well that's Christian's type isn't it?" I grabbed another drink and downed it in one large gulp.

As I walked back around the corner with the liquid confidence pumping through me, I heard Christian talking to his friend and I paused in the doorway when I heard what they were talking about.

"So, is this one crazy too?" asked the guy.

"Seriously man? Did you really just say that? Stop."

The guy laughed in response. "You don't have the best record with this."

I knew I shouldn't but I walked back to the table and downed another two champagne flutes. My inhibitions drifted away like butterflies being released. I walked back, at least I think I walked back but stumble was probably more accurate.

"Hey, where were you?" he asked when I rounded the corner.

I spoke slowly so that I wouldn't slur my words. "Just getting a drink. I milked it so it took a while," I lied.

He raised an eyebrow at me and when I didn't respond he grabbed my hand. "Come on, I'll introduce you to some other people."

"Grrrrreat!" I said a bit too loudly. He laughed and called me a lightweight. I took a hold of his arm to steady myself as we walked to another group.

Christian brought me over to a group of friends deep in conversation. They were all trading stories about parenting, something Christian and I couldn't really participate in. I smiled as they all chatted back and forth. I laughed when they laughed but I was having a hard time focusing. The champagne hit me… and then the anxiety of fucking up this night hit me. The combination made me feel like I was floating above myself.

"I'm just going to use the restroom," I said, excusing myself from the group. At this point, I was full on drunk and I kept my hand lightly touching the wall of the long dark hallway for balance.

I didn't see it, but one of the kids had left a toy on the floor and it caused me to tumble down to the ground.

Laying there on the floor of a dark hallway, I was sucked into a black hole and then transported back to that night. Though there was no one near me, I could feel hands groping at me. While I was only there for a second, it was vivid as hell and I shouted, "Stop! Stop!"

Christian and some of his friends ran to see what the commotion was. Someone turned on the light and I squinted at the overwhelming brightness. Christian pushed past people to get to me. He extended his hand and I clumsily got to my feet.

He whispered in my ear, "Should we go?" And I nodded, completely mortified. I lowered my head, as if that would make me invisible to their stares that felt like lasers burning into me.

As we walked past, his friend from earlier said, "Looks like he got another crazy one."

His voice was upbeat and he looked around to see if anyone laughed in response though everyone just stood in stunned silence.

Christian left my side to approach him. "Jack, you are fucking dickhead. Don't ever talk to me again. And the only thing you should ever say to my girlfriend is an apology."

With that Christian was back by my side, taking my hand quickly and escorting me out of the house. At the car he opened my door and then wrapped his arms around me and we melted into one.

"Christian, I feel awful for causing such a scene. I shouldn't have drunk so much."

"Isa, you have nothing to apologize for. That guy was being an asshole." He leaned his head so it gently touched mine. There was a moment of silence and then he spoke. "I'm so sorry, I'm so sorry." He repeated it over and over softly.

Chapter 21

At this point, I was second guessing if I was getting much out of my sessions with Dr. Price. I liked her, but it felt like I was paying someone just to listen to me complain. If I could make some friends and vent to them, I'd save myself a lot of money. The problem was post-college it isn't so easy to make friends.

I shoved those thoughts aside and walked into my weekly session. The familiarity of it all was reassuring. The chime as I walked into the first door; her warm greeting, followed by the scent of lavender. The muted tones of the decor calmed you instantly.

However, something was different today. Dr. Price, who was normally effortlessly beautiful, seemed a bit unkempt. Her outfit was more casual than she would normally wear. She wasn't wearing her natural makeup showing that her skin was actually rather blotchy. Her hair was pulled back into a ponytail. She looked like she was ready to go shopping at the mall rather than have one of our sessions.

She still looked beautiful but just different than she normally did. One thing remained the same though. She still had on her huge engagement ring that twinkled like a star in the sky. It sat on top of her wedding band, that also looked like it cost a few paychecks. I'd kill for a ring like that.

Dr. Price reached into her mini fridge and offered me a cold seltzer water. She held up a lime and a raspberry. I pointed to the left indicating that I'd like the raspberry flavoring. She popped the can for me and handed it over. The cool bubbles hit my tongue and it was refreshing.

"So how was your date the other night?"

I stuttered because the question took me back. "My... my... I'm sorry, what?"

She adjusted in her seat. "Last time you told me you had a date to a holiday party, correct?"

I thought back to whether or not I had told her this. I didn't recall that. However, it was a minor detail and she takes notes when we speak so I suppose she's more likely to remember things correctly than I am.

"Well, I started seeing that guy again. I feel good about things... I think. We've gotten to a more serious level."

"What does that mean?"

"Well. I met his friends last night, but that was a disaster."

"In what way?" she asked leaning into me, showing she was focused on me.

"I don't know; you know how shy I can be. So, I drank way too much, and then something triggered a flashback and I can't believe it but I started screaming down the hallway. I'm cringing just thinking about it."

"How awful," she said dryly.

I just nodded in response. Even retelling it was mortifying.

"So, you said you were more serious now? Tell me about that."

"Well, the date before we…" I trailed off, not sure if she could fill in the blank, or if it was even a strange thing for me to mention.

"Yes?" she said flatly.

"We were together."

Color drained from her face as her eyes widened.

I continued, "It was all very gentle and loving. We stayed the night together and, at least to me, it solidified my relationship with Christian."

Then she looked visibly ill the more I spoke. I stopped when I thought, Oh god, I think she's about to vomit. She stood up quickly, raising her hand to her mouth. She began making gagging sounds and ran out of the room. I could hear her retching which made my stomach turn. When she walked back in, she was wiping her mouth with a tissue. I was simultaneously grossed out and baffled.

Dr. Price sat back in her seat and said apologetically, "I'm sorry... I'm embarrassed that happed but I'm pregnant!" Her facial expression morphed and she radiated happiness.

I congratulated her.

Her coloring was off and I was worried she'd continue to vomit. I really just wanted to get out of there but our session wasn't done. Dr. Price picked up her notepad and as I made mindless chatter about things that didn't actually bother me, she wrote furiously on her yellow legal pad. Her pen zoomed across the page, aggressively dotting her i's and her facial expression was stern.

As she wrote, all I could think about was how this woman had it all. First of all, she was gorgeous. Second, she must have a loving and healthy relationship that was about to blossom into a little family. Third, she had a successful business that involved being paid hundreds of dollars to pretend to listen to people complain. And the cherry on top, clearly, she was very wealthy judging by the giant diamond on her finger. I tried to push the wave of immature jealousy out of my mind.

When the session was finally done, Dr. Price walked me to her door. "Isabella, I think I'll have to skip next week," she said softly. "I just found out I was pregnant last night and I just want to soak that all in. Doctor's appointments, prenatal yoga, the works! Will you be okay missing a session?"

I said, "Sure." I was thankful that I could skip next week.

When I walked out, the door slammed behind me. I turned around to see she had shut herself in her office. I could hear her retching again. For a split second, I thought to go in and see if she was okay but didn't know if that would blur the lines of our professional relationship. Selfishly, I hoped she wouldn't be vomiting for the next nine months. It surely would make for some awkward therapy sessions.

I messaged Christian to hang out. Normally he was very responsive. I didn't hear from him for a few hours. His reply surprised me with its shortness.

Christian: **Can't tonight. Lots going on.**

More upsetting was the fact that it was the first time he hadn't started his text with 'Hey Gorgeous.' I felt my high-school-girl insecurities rising up and spent time trying to analyze this simple text. Was this because of the party?

Was he embarrassed about me or did his friends convince him to stop talking to me?

Then a tsunami of questions flooded my brain.

Did this mean we were done?

Had he found someone new?

Was he stringing me along to see who he liked better?

We hadn't said we were official. I started to play back what happened at the party. He was so kind to me but maybe his friends talked to him after. Maybe they convinced him that I was crazy. I wish they knew what I had been through. Then maybe they would understand, be empathetic.

The fun part of having anxiety is how easily you can work yourself into a panic over something that could end up being nothing. This wasn't anything new to me. Each interaction we had previously swirled in my head as I analyzed it. From everything else that had happened, this was the only thing off. Things were probably okay, I reassured myself.

Chapter 22

I woke up early, took Winston on a long walk and then decided to go all out on my look for work. If I didn't feel good, at least I could make myself look good. I spent an hour doing my hair and makeup. I put on a hunter green sweater dress with a tan leather belt. To top off the look, I slipped on knee-high tan leather boots.

As I walked through the office, people turned to look. Maybe I had overdone it, but I wanted to feel good about myself and I achieved that goal. It was amazing how spending a little time and effort could improve my self-image. With each step I took, I had a little more pep in my step.

My work computer turned on with a low buzzing sound. They really need to get me a new one. I swear this thing might have been made when I was still in diapers. My cellphone was nearby and I hate to admit that I was obsessively checking to see if I got any texts, but none came in. Once I was able to log on, I had several emails to go through.

I sifted through them to see what was the highest priority. There was an email from Ms. Santiago. When I opened it, I could see it was sent to me and to Troy. The email read:

Please immediately remove my information from your database. Please no longer reach out via phone, email and most importantly home visits. - Trina Santiago

I made a beeline for Troy's cubicle and noticed I turned some heads as I made my way there. Troy was seated at his desk, playing a game on his phone when I placed my hand on his shoulder. He quickly spun around to face me.

His face flashed from fear to shock. "Someone's ready for date night!"

I ignored his comment and got straight to the facts. "Trina Santiago asked us to cut off all contact with her. I'm worried her son is pushing her out of getting the help she needs."

Troy pursed his lips and I could tell he was trying to figure out how to respond. "I already talked with Diane about this. We can ask the police to do a welfare check now. If all looks good, we need to respect her wishes."

My mouth fell open. I couldn't believe he was serious. It is our responsibility to make sure that women who reach out to us are safe. It is well known within our line of work that women who are surrounded by a violent or unhinged family member will often recant their cries for help. The most dangerous time for a woman in that situation is when she tries to leave or to help herself.

Troy himself knows that Lucas is dangerous. He knows that if we abandon Ms. Santiago, especially after Lucas was made aware that she has reached out for help, that she could be putting her life at risk. I pleaded my case once again to Troy but he stood firm for reasons I couldn't figure out.

It was crucial that I got to the bottom of this. We had a moral obligation to help. At this point, I wasn't sure how I would do that but knew dropping the case was not the answer. What if Lucas hurt his mom? Or Talia? We'd have that on our conscience forever and I couldn't live with myself if something happened due to our inaction.

"Troy, I know I told you I knew Lucas from high school. There is more to it."

He raised his eyebrows. "Go on…"

"He's be dating my friend…"

"Isabella! What the hell! You should have told me that."

"I know, I know. I'm sorry. But he's been harassing me."

His eyes widened, he stood from his chair and placed his hand on my shoulder. "Seriously, I know you have a lot of shit going on right now but all this needed to be disclosed right away. We need to go speak to Diane and see how she wants to proceed."

We met with our boss, who decided to take over the case. I spent the rest of the workday alternating between brainstorming how to help Ms. Santiago and checking for messages from Christian. He still hadn't responded by the time I got home. And I hoped Diane had better success with Ms. Santiago than we did. Overall, not a great day.

I twirled my keychain around my finger as I walked to my apartment. Since my day had been so unproductive, I decided I'd be extra productive at home. My plan was to do a few loads of laundry, sweep and do the dishes. My life may be chaotic but I could make my living space less so.

As I put the key in the door, I could hear Winston coming towards it. I walked in, set down my bag and I immediately kneeled down towards the brown and white dog, nuzzling my head into his soft fur. When I lifted my head, I noticed items torn up around the living room. My throw pillows had been opened and the fluff was everywhere.

"Bad Winston!" I scolded. He looked up at me with his big brown eyes. I stood up and surveyed the situation. I dropped my large tote bag right where I stood. Then, I kicked off my shoes angrily as they hit the floor with a thud. It slowly began to hit me that Winston couldn't have done this. Books were taken off the shelves. My desk was in disarray. Someone had been in my home… again.

There was no evidence that anyone had come through my front door based on reviewing the doorbell camera footage. I looked at all my windows and none of them were open. It was a complete mystery on how someone got into the apartment. If I couldn't figure out how they entered, I wouldn't be able to figure out how to keep myself safe. The thought made a shiver run down my spine. My hands trembled as I called my mom.

"I need to stay tonight. Maybe for a while. My place was broken into again."

Her voice was drenched in concern in the way only a mother's voice can be. "Yes, absolutely. Should I drive over to you first? So, you have someone there while you pack up."

I assured her that it wasn't necessary and quickly packed up my things and a small bag for Winston.

I piled my stuff into my ten-year-old Honda. The short drive to my mother's was quick but my anxiety was getting the best of me. I peered around each turn as if monsters lurked around the corner. I glared at drivers near me and felt like everyone was tailing too close. Yes, I was spiraling but who could blame me?

When I arrived at my mother's white ranch house, I picked up Winston, leaving both our bags in the car. I just needed a hug from my mom. She was on the couch watching TV when we entered, a home decorating show loudly playing. I put Winston down as he happily went exploring his new temporary home.

My mother, seeing me, immediately grabbed the remote from the table to turn off the TV. I fell into her arms. Tears sprang to my eyes and before I realized it, I was sobbing. The sound of my own sobs were guttural and the more I cried, the louder they became. The floodgates opened. There was no end in sight to this madness. I was scared and felt alone. The worst part was that I didn't know to what extent this would escalate.

My mother kept one arm around me and the other stroking my hair. I felt like a little kid again but I needed this more than anything. Once my tears subsided, we sat on the couch side-by-side. My mother was always more action oriented so she began suggesting ideas on what we could do to fix this. While her ideas were better than doing nothing, I began to feel hopeless.

"I just need to go rest," I said to her, my voice dripping with worry.

I walked to my old bedroom which was still baby pink from when I lived here a few years back. All my old teenage decor still decorated the walls. The room was a time capsule to everything a teenage girl would have loved ten years ago. A poster of Jesse McCartney; stacks of CDs on the desk and my collection of drugstore makeup. I slipped under the heavy purple and pink comforter, grabbed my eye mask from the nightstand and drifted off to sleep.

When I woke up, it was the next day. My mother had brought all my bags in from the car and placed them in the corner of my room. Small gestures like this always demonstrate the love a mother has for their child. I could also tell she had walked Winston since he peacefully slept next to me instead of licking my face at dawn.

My mother had placed my flute at the edge of my bed, hoping I'd pick it up. Seeing as I didn't have work today or tomorrow, I thought I'd focus some of my energy on playing. I took out my flute and began to play a piece I was working on. It was an Irish song that I instantly connected with. As the notes escaped my instrument, the beauty of the notes moved me to a place far away from a two bedroom in central New Jersey. I was in a grassy open field in Ireland, living my best life. For a few moments, all was good in my world. Then…

Chirp! And just like that I was snapped out of it as I dove for my phone, hoping it was Christian. The screen showed 'Unknown number' and I hoped it was him calling from work.

"Hello?" I said, forcing a calm tone that wasn't reflected in the worry I had.

Instead of it being Christian's voice, it was a deep, raspy voice that I didn't recognize.

"You aren't safe there either."

My body went stiff. For a second, I was frozen while my brain tried to process what was happening. "Who the hell is this?" There was no response. I yelled again, this time louder. "Answer me!" Then I could see they had hung up.

Rage flowed through me and in this state, I shouldn't have but I called Talia. As soon as she picked up the phone, I began to bellow out a tirade.

"Tell your stupid asshole boyfriend, ex-boyfriend, whatever, to leave me the hell alone! I haven't done anything to him and he's practically stalking me at this point! He just called and threatened me and that's the last straw. Tell him if he calls me again, I'm filing a police report!"

I thought she'd respond in anger as well, but she seemed confused. "Isabella, Lucas is right here with me now. We've been watching TV for the past hour. He didn't call you."

"I thought you weren't going to hang out with him anymore?" I demanded.

"I… don't kn—" she stuttered.

"Whatever," I snapped as I hung up the phone.

Was she lying to cover for him? Or was Lucas not the one who had been harassing me? If I knew who was stalking me, I could keep tabs on their whereabouts… but if I had no idea who it was, then I had no idea where they were… or when they were about to strike again.

Chapter 23

Later that night, I was sitting on my bed with Winston at my side. He laid next to me chewing on a blue toy bone. He was hitting the squeaker on it with each bite he took and the high-pitched sound reverberated through the small room.

I heard a knock on the front door and seeing as this wasn't my home, was not going to get up to answer it. It was either someone trying to sell something or convert you. Then I heard my mom's voice, speaking in a few notes higher than normal.

"Oh my god! Talia, you look fantastic."

Two sets of footsteps got louder as they approached my door. My mother lightly knocked and then she was standing before me with Talia.

Awkwardness hung in the air. I had yelled at her, accused her boyfriend of inappropriate, probably even criminal behavior. I wasn't even sure how to start this conversation or what exactly she was here for but she was owed an apology.

She sat on the edge of my bed, like we had done so many times as kids. We'd been in this room getting ready for dances, swaying to music as we did each other's hair and makeup. We'd been here for sleepovers, gossiping about kids in our grade and staying up way too late. We'd been here studying for exams together, trying to make sure we each passed the next day's test. We'd been here, having a bond grow during each of our endless summer adventures, maturing each year as we did so.

Sitting next to me, she hung her head. I could feel the grief emanating off her.

"I need to know," she said softly.

"I know. I think I am ready," I replied. I knew she was right and that it was time. My gulp was audible and then I began to tell her what I had put off for so many months. I recounted that night from the beginning.

Aubrey, Lucas and I were at a party. Talia couldn't make it because she was visiting her grandparents that weekend. We were at a house down at the Jersey shore. It was a nice, small house. It was late September so the beach town was starting to ease into its winter hibernation.

Lucas brought us to a house of some friends from his previous school that we didn't know at all. The vibe was weird. We just didn't feel like we fitted in because we didn't know anyone. We both drank some before we really started to feel like we didn't want to be there.

I said to her, "Can we get out of here? It's lame."

"Yes, please! Let me just go tell Lucas we are leaving. That should be a fun conversation," Aubrey had said back to me.

As she walked away, she swayed a little but I just thought she was a bit buzzed. I didn't know...

Aubrey went and told Lucas that she wanted to go and as she predicted, he was angry. He complained how he hadn't seen this set of friends in a long time, it would be embarrassing if she left, he didn't want to be there without her. And she made her point as well—we didn't know anyone, we were bored, no one was including us, and one of Lucas's 'friends' who was clearly twenty years older than us was creeping us out.

It was getting pretty heated but Aubrey and I were firm that we were going. Lucas was adamant that we couldn't drive though. He told us we were both too wasted.

We didn't listen.

We hopped into her car and blasted music hoping to cleanse the ick from the party out of us.

"Could you believe how stuck up some of those kids were?" I said.

Aubrey took on a mocking tone. "Yeah dude, like come to my two million dollar beach house." We laughed but then she got serious. "I feel bad we left Lucas," she said.

"He will be fine."

I was wrong.

We continued to sing loudly, letting the music ease away our negative emotions. Jewel's Who Will Save Your Soul was playing and we were just belting it out. We were driving down 195 back towards home when Aubrey swerved not to hit an animal. I wasn't sure what she was doing and I grabbed for the wheel trying to correct course. I didn't mean to but I over-corrected. The car did a 180 degree spin and went off the road and crashed into the concrete divider. Aubrey was thrown from the car and was dead on impact.

Back at home, everyone blamed me. They thought I was the cause of the accident. Someone started rumors that I did it on purpose! That I killed her because I was jealous of her and Lucas. In my view, we were both guilty of driving while intoxicated but I would have never done anything to hurt her intentionally. My love for her was and still is overwhelming. The void she left in our lives leaves a sinkhole in everything we do, the mist of 'if Aubrey was here' surrounding us for each important moment, and the smaller ones too.

When I'm done speaking, there is a barrier between us. It's the silence of this secret I've been holding on to for all this time, and now it can either fade away or remain indefinitely. Talia leans into me and puts her head on my shoulder. And just like that I know we have the potential to heal.

We stay like that for a long while savoring a closeness that has been missing for months. I put my hand on her knee to return the intimacy. She lifts her head and gives me a weak smile. We are still hurting; we are forever broken; but we can start to live again.

I don't know how she will take what I was about to say so I hesitate, trying to run the words through my head to get them just right, make my tone more palatable.

"Tal, I know I've said this but I need to say it again. I think you should reconsider dating Lucas. It's not because of Aubrey either… We aren't safe with him around."

Maybe it's because we are in this moment of healing, but she responds better than I expected.

She looks away from me and says, "I'm sorry about the things that are happening to you, and I want to help. I'll do whatever it takes to make you feel safe again but I'm telling you, it isn't Lucas."

I can't tell her that Lucas' mom is afraid of him too. For privacy reasons, I could lose my job for disclosing that. My brain keeps pushing me to say it, a gnawing sensation but I keep pushing it down. So, all I can do is implore her to be safe, as I hand her a keychain mace. She gives me a sideways glance that says, 'really?!' But she takes out her keychain and attaches it to her keyring.

"Did you get one for yourself too?" she asks and I grab my key ring to show her.

"Twinsies," I said but neither of us smile. "My mom sent me a multi-pack."

She reminds me that I still have to look into the self-defense classes and I promise her I will keep looking for something that fits what I need.

Chapter 24

I got dressed for work and message by boss that I have a 'doctor's appointment' and will be in at 10:30 am. My only doctor's appointments are with Dr. Price but I never let my boss and coworkers in on that detail. While I wish people would be more open about therapy, I know people judge so for now I keep it mostly to myself. Hell, I hadn't even told Christian yet.

I enter the parking lot and take out my phone since I'm a few minutes early. I see that I have several missed texts. My heart stops for a second—they are all from Christian.

Christian: **Isa, I'm so sorry. I've had the worst week and I should have reached out.**

Christian: **Can we please talk so I can let you know what is going on?**

Christian: **I miss you.**

Christian: **Please.**

I have one minute before I need to be inside and it isn't enough time to process what I want to say or how I want to handle this. On one hand, I adore being with him and would love to see him. On the other hand, I feel like we have been yo-yoing in and out of contact. It's all so complicated. A response will have to wait until after my session. I grab my flute, which Dr. Price asked me to bring the last time I saw her.

When I walk in, the scent of lavender hangs so thick in the air it makes me choke. I wrinkle my face surprised at how overpowering she has her diffuser going, and then I notice she has several. Her sound machine is pumped high and its buzzing sound makes me feel disoriented.

When she walks to her doorway, she looks downright awful. She must really be suffering with morning sickness, so much that she can't focus on much else. I feel sorry for her and say a little prayer that she doesn't have to experience it for much longer.

"Sit down," she says coolly while standing in the door frame.

The whole situation seems very off to me so I ask her cautiously, "Are you okay?"

She doesn't respond but begins to walk toward her side of the room. I follow behind in silence. Dr. Price goes to her mini fridge and opens a can of seltzer water for me and juts her hand out to me signaling for me to take it.

I place the water on the small wooden side table. "I brought my flute!" I say with forced cheer.

Again, she doesn't respond. She sits in her seat, her notepad out and writes without looking at me. I'm unsure of what to do so I open the case and begin to play. The small room is filled with the beautiful musical notes of a flute and the harsh white noise masking most of it.

This is incredibly awkward and I don't know what to do, so I sit down and take a large swig of the water. Then I slowly put my flute away and close the container. She continues to stare at me and I feel unsettled. I take another large swig of water.

"How do you feel?"

I say a silent thank you that we are going to get back to our normal session.

I begin to tell her how I'm so worried that Christian has been pulling away from me. "I thought I was falling in love with him so it's painful and I'm just incredibly confused."

She glares at me. "What could possibly be confusing to you? He's married. He's probably spending time with his wife… where he should be." She smirks, looking satisfied at cutting me down.

I shift in my seat wondering what is happening right now.

From some part of me that I didn't know existed, I find some courage. "Listen, I don't know what is happening here but you are my therapist. Whatever happened in your past, can't affect how you interact and help me."

"Isabella, I can't help you or any other patient for that matter when the choice is made to do something unethical. I just simply won't do it."

"What are you saying? You can't meet with me anymore?"

"I'm saying I don't think it is best if we continue. We will meet one more time to close out what we have worked on for the past year. I will also bring you recommendations for therapists that I think will be a good fit for you. Let's meet again in two weeks so I have time to research who would be a good match."

I shake my head disapproving of this whole situation. She looks back at me unfazed.

"You didn't even listen to me play. You asked me to bring my flute." I realize that my statement is childish and petty as soon as it slips from my lips.

"Bring it to our final session, please. I'd love to hear you play," she said dryly. She picked up her laptop and began typing. After a moment she said, "So sorry, but my next availability isn't until March 1st. I know that is really far—"

"Sure whatever. I'll be there." I grab my stuff and walk out, way before our session was supposed to be done. There is a young man sitting in the lobby and I realize that she had no intention of having a full session with me today. I look at the young man and say, "You're in bad hands here." He looks at me confused but stays in his seat. I slam the door on my way out.

What a total bitch! I can't believe I've essentially been dumped by my therapist. Is that even a thing?!

The rage is bubbling up in me and I am feeling vindictive. Plots of revenge run through my mind. Most are too extreme and are just to pacify my anger, with no real intention of seeing them through. I come to an acceptable plan of action. My mind started going a mile a minute with all the venom I will put onto every review site she is on.

My mind is so clogged with this that I completely forget to message Christian back. It's the last thing on my mind. I needed to head to work and hoped the change of location will erase the feelings on negativity. Suddenly I feel tired and my vision blurs a bit. *I'll just close my eyes for a minute*, I think to myself.

There is a soft knocking on my window. When I don't respond, it gets louder..

Finally I wake up, with Dr. Price standing there outside my car. It takes me a moment to realize where I am and why I am here. "Yeah, yeah. I'm fine. Sorry," I replied as I started up the engine. My car dashboard says it is 11:52 am.

"Shit!" I said aloud and despite still feeling woozy, I quickly speed off towards the office.

Chapter 25

After the session, I arrived at work and sat at my desk unsure of what to do first.

I could hear Troy call to me from his cubicle, "Are you going to answer that?"

I had gone into a daze several times, so deep in thought that I didn't hear the phone ringing right on my desk. I pick up the phone and there was static at the other end.

"Hello?" I repeat several times.

Sometimes women call us and are in danger and can't speak. I begin to use the code that some women recognize as a way to call for help that can be undetected by their abuser.

"Are you calling to order a pizza?"

No response.

More static.

As I am about to hang up, a husky voice that sounds unreal bellows from the receiver. "I know what you did with my husband. Little home wrecking slut."

Slamming down the phone, I spun in my chair looking around the office. No, the call is not coming from inside the house.

Diane approached my cubicle. "Just checking in. I thought you would have been here sooner. Everything okay?"

While she tried to sound concerned, I knew she was disappointed that I came in late. "I'm sorry. I wasn't feeling well after my appointment. It took me awhile to get myself together. I promise it won't happen again." She gave me a sympathetic smile and walked away.

After a full day of work, I was still fuming. The prank calls, my boss being unhappy with me, the ups and downs with Christian and mostly the situation with Dr. Price. There was far too much on my plate right now and I couldn't cope with all the tension.

I hopped into my bed, with my Chromebook resting on my lap. The warmth from the device felt like a hug. Winston soon jumped up to sit alongside me. I ran my fingers through his soft fur and felt the instant calming effects relax my tense muscles.

I entered Dr. Price's name into the Google search bar wondering if I can find any dirt on her. Nothing interesting comes up. She organized a food drive in town a few years back and she's featured in another article about therapy during the pandemic.

Then I find several professional sites that she is on. I'm determined to bring her review rating down for what she has done here. I'm literally at the lowest point of my life, literally drowning in depression at times and now she's left me with no help. I can't fucking get over how wrong this is.

I opened a Google doc and draft a message. I decided to write it now while my mind is fresh with ideas but planned to post it at the right time. If I did it now, maybe she wouldn't meet me for our final session and I needed those recommendations. With everything happening now, I didn't trust myself without the help of a therapist.

I began to type.

Dr. Price is so unprofessional that she should no longer be able to practice. She appears disheveled each time we meet, and if she can't get her shit together, how can she help you with yours? She is always distracted and looking at her phone, while you are paying top dollar to have her pretend to listen to you. Worst of all, she has the audacity to abandon clients who are in severe need of help. She's practicing so recklessly that lives are at risk. Avoid at all costs.

I reread it and am pleased with what I wrote. I think it explains the situation I experienced and gives fair warning to anyone else in this situation. They say writing a letter can be therapeutic so maybe by the time our next session rolls around I'll decide to delete this.

Since I'm at the computer, I decided to Google local self-defense classes. This time I have a better idea of what I am looking for. I'd like it to be run by a woman, preferably someone with a background of working with people who have already experienced trauma. I think I'd also like it to be one on one or at least a small group, in case I have another episode.

After some searching, I find something that fits the bill. It's about forty minutes from my house but seeing as it meets all my criteria, I decided to sign up. I shot off a quick text to invite Talia but she quickly messaged back that she was unavailable.

Chapter 26

February 2024

I opened up Christian's texts and reread them. Everything I started to write, I erased. The insecurities and uncertainty about it all made me second guess everything and I really didn't know how I wanted to proceed. Finally, I thought I should at least see him one more time, even if it was just for closure.

I sat on a park bench waiting for him. I shivered slightly, partly from the weather and partly from nerves. As he walked towards me, I noticed he looked absolutely haggard. I stood to greet him and he immediately enveloped me in a hug. His head rested on top of mine and I could feel him breathing deeply, taking in the scent of my apple shampoo.

As I tried to think of what to say, he began first.

"Isa. Isa… I'm so sorry. Can we walk and I'll explain everything?"

I nodded gently and as we started on the path, he took my hand in his. His large hand nearly swallowed mine whole.

"I've had probably one of the worst weeks I've ever had. It was almost impossible to cope. I had to take time off from work which I never do. I wasn't really in touch with anyone so I could process it all." He looked over at me as he spoke, trying to gauge my reception of what he was saying. "Listen, I haven't seen my ex in five months and she's been contacting me multiple times a day. She is saying all this crazy shit, shit that is impossible. I've been trying to get a restraining order and I've been trying to get my lawyer to hurry the hell up with this divorce. It has just been a very stressful time."

"She's been calling me."

He stopped walking and let go of my hand. He turned towards me in complete shock.

"How did she get my information? She's been to my house; she's called me at work. I'm scared."

"God, I'm so sorry I brought you into this. When I first contacted you, I was just hoping for... well, a distraction. I didn't think we'd click and end up seeing each other as often as we had. I can't tell you how sorry I am."

Christian looked pained as he spoke about it and I reached over to stroke his arm. We made contact and then he kissed me. Deeply. I was a little startled by this but quickly fell into it. Our arms wrapped around each other and then he moved his hand to my head. In a low growling whisper he implored, "Can we get out of here?"

My eyes locked with his and I just nodded. We walked the two blocks back to his place, our hands interlocked. The anticipation of what was coming made heat rise through me and quickened my pace.

The sun was lower to the horizon, causing water-colored streaks of pinks, yellows and oranges across the sky. The setting of the sun brought colder temperatures and he brought me closer to him. When we turned the corner, his place came into view.

"Shit!" he screamed.

I looked to where he was looking at and noticed it too. He dropped my hand and walked over to his car. The little bit of day light left revealed a long key mark through the length of his new Audi. Christian lowered his head and slowly passed his hand over his face. Then he let out a long, slow exhale.

"I don't even know what to do anymore." He said it not to me, just aloud.

The romantic moment between us passed. We had an understanding of each other though. We both had toxic people in our lives that caused major stressors. Maybe that's why we were drawn to each other in the first place.

"Let's *actually* get out of here," I said.

He turned his head toward me.

"I mean it. Let's just pack a bag and get the hell out of here. Go someplace beautiful for the weekend. Get our heads straight. And if that isn't possible, we can at least get a tan and some cocktails."

He didn't even need time to think about it.

"Absolutely." He leaned over and kissed my forehead.

I closed my eyes as he did and absorbed the warmth of it. Fucked up situation or not, I wanted to be with him. "So, I signed up for this self-defense class tonight. It's a bit of a hike from here and Talia can't make it, but I thought you could accompany me."

He hesitates so I ask him what is on his mind.

"Do I have to act as the attacker? I don't think I'd be comfortable with that."

I shake my head. "You could just come with me. Sitting in the lobby might be a good time to buy tickets for our getaway. And we could get dinner after. It's near Rutgers, this woman offers one on one self-defense classes for college students."

Christian agrees and we make the drive up north.

A woman who introduces herself as Sarah welcomes me in. Christian takes a seat in the waiting room. Sarah asks me what my motivation for starting self-defense training is. I vaguely tell her that I'm nervous because of some odd things that have been happening around me. I don't go into details and she doesn't press me. We spend the first fifteen minutes just talking about how she structures her class and the importance of taking a course like this one. I like her calm demeanor and already know I made the right choice by selecting her as my instructor.

She is able to walk me through some simple moves that we practice over and over. I look back at Christian who looks up from his phone and gives me a big smile and a thumbs up. When the hour is up, Sarah walks me to the exit and Christian extends his hand to her. "Thanks for doing this. It is important work." I beam at him.

Once we are in the car, he turned to me and said, "So we are all set. We leave tomorrow morning, just a quick one-night trip to Florida. Let's grab a quick dinner and then get packing!"

We are both excited at our sudden impulsivity and it is a welcome distraction.

Chapter 27

The next morning, we were at the Trenton airport waiting for a flight to Florida. We'd escape the cold New Jersey winter for a few days in the sun. I'd always been a nervous flier, so I sat in the small waiting area with my leg bopping up and down a mile a minute.

He gently placed his hand on my knee and leaned into whisper, "It's going to be okay."

And I knew it would.

We had two days ahead of us and because this was all so new to us, time seemed to slow down. On our first day, we dropped our bags in the room and then headed straight to the pool. Since this was a last-minute trip, I hadn't bought anything new so I was feeling a bit self-conscious in my old bathing suit.

I went to grab two chairs and Christian went to get drinks. He was walking over towards me, a frozen pina colada in one hand and a beer in the other. I noticed he looked to the side and his face flashed fear for a brief second.

"What was that all about?" I asked as he handed me my cold drink. The frosty pineapple and coconut combination was so refreshing in this sweltering heat.

"Nothing." He chugged his beer.

"It didn't look like nothing. Come on. Tell me!"

"I could have sworn I saw my ex, but I think she's gotten into my head so much. Forget it. I was wrong. Let's just enjoy the day."

I could tell he didn't want to talk about it so I didn't bring it up again. But I definitely was looking around more, not that I even knew what she looked like.

"If you are right, if she's following you places—you need to get a restraining order. And show me what she looks like. I need to know what to look out for, right?"

Christian quickly downed his beer and looked at me. "I don't have any pictures of her on my phone anymore. I try not to think about her."

"Okay so what does she look like?"

"She's short but she likes wearing heels. She's got dark brown hair. Average build."

He went to get another drink. In short succession he'd had four. He began to talk a bit more loudly and was a bit handsy with me. I wasn't even close to being buzzed.

"Let's get into the pool," I coaxed, hoping the cold water would snap him out of it. As we walked, he placed his hand on my bottom. "There are kids around," I whispered and he removed his hand.

"Sorry, you just look so good."

"I think it is just your beer googles."

He furrowed his brown. "Hey, don't talk like that about yourself. You are gorgeous—beer or no beer."

In the pool, I stood against the wall and he pressed his body right to mine. I could feel how much he wanted me and I began to grow hot. He leaned in to kiss me and I allowed him to slip his tongue into my mouth. I pulled away, eager for what I knew was coming next. I leaned into his ear and nibbled the bottom for just a second and then whispered, "Let's go back to the room."

He didn't even respond; he took my hand and walked us quickly out and back to our room.

When we got there, he locked the door behind us and gazed at me as if he was going to devour me right there. He placed his hands on my head and brought me in for a deep kiss. My hands manically roamed over his back. Slowly, he slipped one strap down, paused, then slowly trailed his finger down my shoulder releasing the other strap. He was teasing me and it was making flashes of heat pulsate through me.

He flipped me around so I was facing away from him and unlatched the back of my bikini top. His arms reached around and started at my stomach. He was slowly moving them up my body and I yearned for him to arrive where I knew he was heading.

Then suddenly there was a loud pounding at the door.

A low growling, "Fuuuuck," came from Christian.

"Yeah?" I called towards the door, annoyed.

"Mandatory security check!"

I quickly grabbed my top and put it back on and Christian walked to open the door. He turned back to make sure I was ready before he opened it.

"What's this all about?" he asked.

"We got a call about your room. Mind if we look around?"

Christian looked back to me and I shrugged. "Go right ahead."

We awkwardly stood in the corner still dripping from the pool as they peered into each space of the room.

Finally, the guard turned toward us. "Sorry to waste your time. Seems like it was a prank call." He politely said goodbye, though I could hear the tension in his voice.

Once we shut the door behind them, I asked, "What the hell was that all about?"

He rolled his eyes and shook his head. He mumbled a string of expletives under his breath before saying, "I think she is here. I think she followed us here."

A long slow exhale released from me like letting the air escape from a balloon.

Our two days had an air of unease but we made the best of it. We had the chance to spend focused time on each other. Right before our flight back, I felt assured that this thing with Christian could be something special once we worked out all the issues in our own lives.

As we sat in the Orlando airport, my nerves were a wreck again.

I turned to him. "I know you want to wait until things clear up, start things off on the right foot and all but who knows when that will be. I'd like to be your girlfriend… now."

He laughed. "I already thought you were." Then he pressed his lips to mine and the familiar wave of heat went through me again.

"So, to be clear, you aren't seeing anyone besides me… and your wife." All the fellow passengers around us turned their heads and we broke into giggles.

"She's kidding!" he loudly pronounced and he winked at me. "My girlfriend here is a real comedian."

The flight back was a short two hours but with my fear of flying it felt like a full day. Despite all the places I had traveled, I had never learned to get over this fear. My muscles tensed and my heart fluttered. Christian tried to make conversation to distract me and it helped a little.

"Wednesday is Valentine's Day. Do you want to be my Valentine?"

"I'd love to," I said smiling back at him.

He grabbed my hand. "I'll take you for a nice dinner. I want to make up for all the drama this weekend."

He went on about different things we could do and I listened nodding, not fully processing everything he said.

Panic was clouding my mind. I wasn't only worried about the flight… I was worried Christian was hiding something from me—that his ex-wife had been stalking us for a while now and had no plans of easing up.

Chapter 28

You'd think a weekend in a sunny place with a gorgeous man would help your state of mind, but it didn't. I could feel myself starting to slip away again. Insecurities racked my mind. It seemed, no matter how much I improved myself, there was still this hurt little girl inside of me. I had no idea how to heal her and she continued to haunt my adulthood.

Right now, my life consisted of a job I enjoyed, supportive mother, a decent social life and a budding romance. Yet, when I was sinking into this hole, all I could feel was how unworthy I felt as a child. That nagged at me— that none of this was enough. I wasn't enough.

I slogged through a day of work, weak from not eating for twenty-four hours and then returned home. My mother wasn't home yet. I threw back a handful of pills with a shot of whiskey in hopes of sleeping for a long, long time. I should be more careful but in that moment, I just wanted to sleep.

Tuesday morning and my alarm went off at 8:00 am. I had slept since 5:30 last night. Gratitude to be alive washed over me. I would try to make the most of this day. I just had to get through one day at a time.

At the foot of my bed lay Winston, without a care in the world, completely oblivious to the issues I was having. Noticing that I was awake, he got up, walked over to me and plopped down with his body interlocking into mine.

"You are such a good boy!" I cooed, petting his soft fur. "I promise I won't do that again," I said and he licked my hand in approval.

Work was slow and I flipped through my photos on my phone from the weekend. I had told Christian I would go through the many, many photos we took and send over my favorites.

Troy came up behind me. "You look tanned!"

I told him about the trip to Florida and I showed him some of the pictures I had taken.

"Look at these two love birds! It looks like you had a good time!"

"It was good, but some crazy shit happened."

"Ohhh, let me set my email away message." I laughed and he parked himself next to me. "Do tell!"

I began to recount what happened: Christian thinking he saw his ex-wife, someone calling security, at the most delicate of moments and my almost one-hundred percent sure suspicion that she was the cause of that.

Troy listened in sheer shock.

"Good drama, right?"

"Isabella, I don't ever tell you what to do, other than pick up your phone when you are in la-la-land, but you can't take this lightly. You and I both have listened to enough true crime shows to know this situation is not okay and I really don't want you to be the subject of a podcast I listen to one day. Please do something—call the police, a restraining order?"

I brought my thumb to my mouth and began to chew away at what little nail was left. "Yeah, yeah I will."

After he went back to his workspace, I sent over the pictures to Christian. He immediately began hearting each one. Soon my phone chirped.

Christian: **So where is our next adventure?**

I thought about this for a minute. What were some good spots that we could easily do in a weekend?

Me: **We could go into Philly for the weekend.**

Christian: **We aren't tourists in Philly. We basically are from Philly.**

Me: **Fair enough, so you pick. Where to?**

Christian: **Well, you know Jamaica is tops on my list but we would need more time than a weekend…. Hmm… My parents have a cabin in Vermont. It's very cozy this time of year. Blankets, fireplace, wine.**

Me: **That literally sounds perfect.**

Christian: **I'll get planning. Miss you.**

Right before I was leaving my boss approached me. "Hey, can you come to the meeting room for a second?"

I stood up and adjusted my skirt. A laundry list of minor offenses went through my head, like how I had just spent the last hour looking at photos on my phone. Shit, I thought, I am about to be fired.

She closed the door behind us. Not good. I sat down at the small meeting table, placing my hands underneath my legs so she can't see them trembling. I really, really needed this job.

Diane spoke first, "I know you have been through a lot lately. More than anyone should have to endure. And I wanted to compliment you."

I looked up quickly to meet her gaze.

"You are doing the very best that can be asked of you at the moment. So, you should be proud that you have been able to start to get your life back on track. However, I've noticed that you seem distracted often. Is that a fair assessment?" She tilted her towards me waiting for me to respond.

"Yes, Diane. That's fair," I admitted. Both she and I knew I desperately needed this job. We both knew I also cared about my work and did want to do well. I swallowed deeply. "I promise to be more focused."

She took a deep sigh. "Listen, this isn't my place to say this but maybe you should talk to someone. They can help you work through this. I know once you get to a better place that you'll be able to focus more on your work too."

I nodded. "Yeah, maybe I'll look into it."

"There is no shame in therapy, Isabella. I know you've often recommended it to clients."

She was right of course. I often recommended it. Yet, I couldn't come to admit to those around me that I was and had been seeing someone. It was like if I said it aloud, everyone would know that I was damaged.

I left our brief meeting knowing I needed to get my head back into the game at work. Not just to appease Diane. I owed it to my clients too. They were depending on me to get them through difficult situations and I couldn't do that if I was consumed with my own issues.

Chapter 29

It was Valentine's Day morning and I was looking forward to what was in store for me. Christian kept texting me in the previous days hinting at what we would do but overall, it was a surprise.

My phone buzzed and lit up with the message:

Christian: **Meet me at 7:00 pm at Sayen Gardens.**

Interesting choice I thought. The grounds were beautiful but it was mid-February. It would be cold and dark.

After my talk with Diane, I knew I had to put the date out of my mind for now and focus on my work. I quickly typed that I'd see him there, powered down my phone and placed it in my desk drawer, not trusting myself with distractions. For the next several hours, I made calls and responded to emails. Towards the end of the day Diane stopped by and complimented how much more focused I was.

When 7:00 pm arrived, I pulled into the nearly empty parking lot and walked over to the gazebo where we agreed to meet. It was cold and I shivered uncontrollably as I sat there. I tried pacing in the gazebo to warm up but it didn't seem to help. After what seemed like forever, I realized I hadn't powered up my phone since leaving work.

I turned it on to see if Christian had messaged me to say he'd be late but nothing appeared. After a few more minutes passed, I decided I'd try to call him but as I was scrolling through my contacts list, I felt something hard hit me. I spun around trying to see what it was but it was too dark.

"Hello?!" I called into the darkness. "Who's there?"

Of course, no one responded. Again, something hit me in the back. I was being pelted with rocks. I was in no mood to find out who it was, I took off toward my car and sped home.

I quickly ran into my house and locked the door behind me. I was starting the kettle to make tea as I desperately needed to warm up, when my phone rang. The screen read Christian. I rolled my eyes, furious at how this night had unfolded.

"What?" I barked into the phone.

"Isabella, I'm so sorry. I don't even know how to explain this."

"Well, you better figure it out quickly because I am so pissed off right now."

"I didn't stand you up. Not intentionally. I was on my way to Sayen Gardens. I had a big bouquet of roses for you. I have them here. I got a phone call that my mother was in an accident and was in the hospital. I raced over and when I got there, I was told no one with that name was there. I called her phone and she was home safe and sound. I'm sure you can figure out where this is going. I'm so sorry."

"It's fine," I said, knowing this wasn't his fault. I couldn't blame him for his estranged wife's crazy behavior. "I don't want to sound crazy but maybe we should be able to track each other on our phones, for safety purposes," I said cautiously, not sure if that was going overboard.

"Yeah, that sounds good to me," he said and agreed to set it up the next time we were together.

The next morning when I opened my door to go to work, the roses were in three separate vases. I picked them up and placed them on the kitchen counter, admiring their beauty and then the thought of the night before made me cringe. I decided to bring the roses to work and give them out to coworkers.

Chapter 30

March 1, 2024 Early morning

Today was my last session with Dr. Price. The rush of both anger and anxiety was vomit inducing. I had my drafts ready to post on different review sites. This was the moment I could have been mature and decide not to post. However, I chose not to take the mature route. She deserved to be exposed for how easily she dropped clients in need.

Click! Click! Click!

I posted on four different sites. It was a satisfying feeling and hoped that my reviews would convince people to stay away from this disgrace of a doctor.

Right after I posted, I saw a text from Dr. Price. I momentarily froze, thinking she saw my reviews. However, the text read:

Dr. Price: **Remember to bring your flute. I'd love to hear you play again.**

Whatever. I patted Winston on the head and then grabbed my case. I was eager to get this over with and find my next therapist.

Walking into the office for one last time felt strange. The lavender scent wasn't there this time, which struck me as odd. I'd wished for this last time be to like all the rest. I had never been good at goodbyes or having things end. It always left a sadness that would linger for far too long. The idea that you'd never have this exact experience again felt like a void that couldn't be filled.

I was expecting to see Dr. Price disheveled as she had the last two times. This time, she looked put together and she was sporting a tan. Her hair, makeup and clothes made her look impeccable. I tried to see if I could notice a baby bump but I saw none. *It is still early*, I thought to myself.

Dr. Price motioned for me to sit without saying a word. She walked over to her mini fridge, popped a seltzer for me and handed it over. I thanked her but there was venom in my voice so I suppose that is why she didn't reply.

There was a pounding sound. It sounded like it was coming from next door. "Do you hear that?" I asked.

"Must be something going on in the other office," she remarked casually.

She went over to the door and turned on her noise machine at full blast which blocked those waiting in the lobby from hearing our conversation. I placed my flute at my feet and she sat across from me, just staring at first.

I took a long sip of the seltzer water. "So…." I said.

"How has your return to work been?"

"Okay," I replied.

"Isabella, are you okay? You look pale. Maybe take another sip of water?"

I did.

I could still hear the pounding but it was muffled by the white noise machine. What was that?

She was talking to me; I could see her mouth moving but she sounded like she was underwater.

I furrowed my brow.

"You said you'd give me recommendations for other therapists. I'd really like to get something set up as soon as possible." At least that was what I was trying to say, but I heard myself produce a jumble of words, slowly drawing out each syllable.

I began squinting. Something didn't feel right. I shook my head, as if to sweep away the cobwebs in my mind. It didn't help. I thought I heard a call for help. Maybe I was imagining it.

"Did you hear that?" I asked groggily.

She ignored my question.

"We haven't seen each other in a while. What have you been up to?" she repeated.

"I uh, I went…" I couldn't recall what I had done recently. Not a single thing. My eyelids felt very heavy as if there were small weights trying to pull them shut. It became hard to resist trying to close them.

"We uh, went to… went to…" There was no memory there. My eyes shut and it felt like such a relief to no longer have that weight pressing down on me. My head felt too heavy for my neck to hold up. I felt like I was swirling and swirling down a black hole.

Then… nothing.

Chapter 31

The moment my eyelids reopened, I froze. I didn't know where I was or how I got there. Every muscle in my body felt rock solid as I lay on the floor. My mind and eyes were the only thing functioning. My gaze darted around sending signals to my brain that it could not process.

I was laying on the floor, staring up at the fluorescent lights on the ceiling. The lighting made me momentarily think I was in a hospital bed but then I could feel my cold flute in my hand.

Slowly, I swiveled my head around and I was definitely not in the hospital. Crimson splatter was everywhere, like I was dropped into a Jackson Pollock painting.

The confusion was disorienting and I was convinced I must be asleep, trapped in a nightmare. I raised my hand and swiftly smacked myself. It stung. This was real. But where was I? And how did I get here? Most importantly—what the hell happened to me?

I took in the small desk in the corner, and the two chairs. Everything was splattered a scarlet red. Then I noticed the poster, 'Be Kind to Your Mind.' On the wall, thick, red streams flowing down it. A soft buzzing sound echoed around me. The lavender diffuser now going but unable to mask the metallic smell of blood.

Then, everything started to click. Though everything was beyond my comprehension, there was one thing I was sure of now. I was in my therapist's office, lavender diffuser and white noise machine still going. However, Dr. Price was not in the room.

I may have laid there for several minutes but it felt like an eternity as I tried to process what was going on, to make some sense of this scene. When I finally had it in me to move, I wasn't even sure where I'd go or what I'd do. There was blood all around me.

I didn't know if it was mine, though I didn't feel any pain. And if it wasn't mine, whose was it?

"Dr. Price?" I called out weakly. "Hello? Dr. Price?... Anyone? Help, please…" My voice trailed off, lacking the energy to scream despite desperately wanting to.

Get yourself together, I told myself. I needed to figure this out. Someone must have attacked us while we were in our session. I could only think of one person who would want to hurt us—Lucas.

He was the common thread between us and he had revenge on his mind for a while now.

"Dr. Price?" I called out several times, each time louder and more frantic.

There was only silence.

I sat up and dug my phone out of my pocket. 6:12 pm Somehow, I had been laying on the floor for about seven hours, with no memory of what happened.

Chapter 32

March 1, 2024 Late in the evening

At 6:14 pm, my trembling fingers dialed 911 to report what had happened. I huddled behind the chair until I heard the door to the office open.

"Shiiiit," an officer said, drawing out the word.

My eyes darted from person to person, trying to take in the situation, unsure of what to do next.

EMTs entered the room behind the police. I started to feel safe once they arrived. They spoke to me in a calm voice, one EMT repeating, "It's going to be okay."

The full memory of it isn't all there but I recall I was taken in an ambulance to the local hospital where my mother was there waiting for me.

The first thing I thought was that I was thankful for having a room alone. I knew once I processed what had happened, the tears would come and wouldn't stop. But for now, there was just confusion and fear. Those emotions took hold of me and wouldn't let go.

In that unfamiliar room, I curled into a ball and slept for countless hours.

A pudgy nurse with short curly black hair walked Christian into my room. She called over her shoulder, "You only have five minutes."

"Hey, I rushed over as soon as I heard. Your mom contacted me." I looked over at my mother who smiled sheepishly. She stood from her chair and let us know she'd be going to the cafeteria to grab a cup of coffee.

"It's good to see you." My voice cracked.

Christian reached for my hand. "How are you?"

I just stared at him.

"Sorry. Stupid question. It will all work out. Once they catch Lucas, he will spend decades in jail for attacking you. And I told my ex yesterday that I was in love with you, that you are my girlfriend and that she needed to stop contacting me. I haven't heard from her in forty-eight hours. She normally texts me a few times an hour. Hate to say it under these circumstances but both our issues are working out and we can finally just focus on each other."

"Cut the trauma bond, and just bond."

"Yeah," he said softly and then kissed my hand.

"Do they know for sure Lucas did this to me? Like did they catch him?"

He paused. "I just assumed. I wish I had been there, Isa. Where did he attack you?"

There was a soft rap on the door and the pudgy nurse had returned. She tapped her watch indicating it was time to reclaim Christian. I was terrified to be left alone but she insisted he needed to go. He turned back to look at me one last time at the doorway.

"Bye," I said solemnly. He blew a kiss and was gone.

Several minutes later, a female officer knocked on my door and entered. She was in full uniform including her gun. I had never seen an officer on duty without a gun, but just the sight of it while I lay in the hospital bed, felt jarring to me.

"Isabella Frank?"

I nodded. I was in no mood to talk. All I could think about was sleep in this moment.

"I'm Officer Cole. I'm here to ask you a few questions." In her hand she held a small notepad and pen.

I absolutely wanted to help find whoever did this to me and Dr. Price.

When I tried to speak, my voice was weak and almost inaudible.

"Lucas."

Confusion spread over Officer Cole's face.

"Look into Lucas. I think he did this."

"Did what?"

I didn't understand her question. My head jerked from side to side trying to shake out the confusion.

"Hurt us."

Her voice showed that she was getting a bit frustrated with me.

"Who is us?"

I must have looked at her like she was crazy. Didn't anyone prep her on what happened so I didn't have to fill her in on the details?

"Isabella, I spoke with the doctor's, all the tests came back and they cleared you to leave. I've been given orders that I need to take you down to the station for questioning."

"But... I don't have anything I can possibly tell you."

"You were there," she said stupidly.

"Yes. But I... I blacked out."

Officer Cole lowered her head to hide her reaction.

"I blacked out." I repeated the phrase, forcing myself to portray confidence, as if I said it enough, she would find it to be the truth.

It didn't work. I was soon in the back seat of a police car, headed straight to the station with the hospital ID bracelet still on my wrist. I twisted the band around and around, watching the letters blend together as I moved it at a faster and faster pace.

Chapter 33

"The 'Blackout Girl' is in the interrogation room."

"Pff!" laughed the other officer. "Is that what we are calling her now?"

"We've got a straight up psycho in there. I've never seen a crime scene so gruesome. That is one messed up chick in there."

Footsteps then…

The two officers sat down across from me and the interrogation began.

They quickly got me to rise to anger and I let my emotions get away from me.

I pounded on the table, leaving my bloody palm print on the table.

It was in that moment that I realized I was completely fucked.

Chapter 34

I had been in that interrogation room for several hours. No sleep, no food. With my depression, sometimes I could cope with those things but the addition of this overwhelming stress made it too much. At this point, I was delirious.

"Listen, I think I need a lawyer."

He tilted his head. "Are you sure?" His voice softened.

I knew they didn't want me to lawyer up. It would be easier to trip me up if I didn't have anyone advising me. However, it is impossible to trip me up, because I honestly have no clue what happened in that room. One minute I was in therapy, the next I was laying in the middle of a bloodbath.

"I want a lawyer," I repeated firmly. "And I want to go home."

Their eyes widened like they couldn't believe I had said that.

"Ms. Frank, you do know that you can't just go home."

In fact, I hadn't realized that but I was starting to understand that I was way, way out of my league and I needed some help.

Aloud, I began to work through what I thought was happening. "Okay, so my therapist and I are attacked in her office and you're keeping me in custody?!"

"Ms. Frank, cut the crap."

I wrapped my fingers on the table manically. I needed a method to get this anxiety released from my body so I could have a clear head.

"Let me talk to Dr. Price. We will clear this up."

Officer Rossi glared at me as he said, "Dr. Price is dead. She was bludgeoned to death and stuffed into her office closet.... Ms. Frank, if this wasn't clear, you are our main suspect."

Chapter 35

When my lawyer arrived, we sat in a private room.

"My name is Nicola McDermont." She was dressed in an ill-fitting navy pants suit. Her long red hair was pulled back to show her porcelain skin. She smiled at me softly and showed me compassion. Immediately I could tell that I liked her.

She too asked me to repeat what happened. "It's crucial that you always be honest with me and tell me everything, from start to finish. Once I have a full picture, we can work together to formulate the best way to defend you."

With that, she pulled open an iPad with a keyboard, all set to type my response. Despite the fact that I couldn't recall a single thing that happened, I recounted why I started seeing Dr. Price, how long I had been seeing her and some of the changes that I had seen over the last few sessions. I ended with the reason I was told that this would be our final session.

"And what about the final session? Tell me from start to finish."

"They said Dr. Price was dead. Is that... true?"

She nodded her head.

"And they think I did it?" I said in disbelief.

She nodded again.

I sucked in a big breath and let it out slowly.

"And you?... Do you think I did it?"

"Isabella, I am your lawyer. I am here to defend you no matter what. If you tell me the truth, I will work to have the truth come out to the judge, jury and to the public. I'm on your side and will do everything I can to defend you."

I paused to consider her answer. She didn't respond that she thought I was innocent. However, she seemed genuine and I did trust what she was saying to me.

"Okay. Let's continue. I walked into Dr. Price's office today. I had my flute with me because I was trying to re-teach myself how to play. She said it could be therapeutic. I sat down and she asked me a few questions and I started to feel unwell."

"Unwell? How?" she interrupted. She was typing so fast. The quick sound on the keyboard was distracting and disorienting to me.

"Well, I suddenly felt weak, confused. My eyelids became so heavy that I could no longer keep them open and then I blacked out. I woke up in a horror scene. I have no idea what happened in between. Not a sight, not a sound, nothing."

"Did you have any reason to hurt your therapist?"

"I didn't hurt her!"

"I need to know if you had a *reason* to hurt her, things the cops might try to use as a motive."

"She abruptly ended our professional relationship for what she claimed where moral reasons. I'm dating someone who is in the middle of a divorce. She said she could no longer work with someone in that situation and wanted to meet this last time to recommend new therapists and bring closure—we had been meeting for over a year. Up until recently I liked her well enough." I paused for a moment. "Yeah, so I was upset about her ending things. I left several bad reviews trying to expose how unprofessional she had become. Nothing unhinged—normal complaint you'd see on these types of sites."

"So, she ended your professional relationship. As far as I know, that is pretty unheard of. How did that make you feel?"

"Mad as hell."

Nicola stopped typing at that moment and looked up at me to evaluate my facial expression. She didn't try to hide her surprise.

"But not mad enough to kill her," I added quickly.

Chapter 36

With my lawyer by my side, I was forced back into the interrogation room.

Both Officer Rossi and Officer Clark sat across from me again. Officer Clark leaned over and pressed record on the device.

"We'd like you to explain to us a few things we found at the scene."

I laughed, though I shouldn't have. I always laughed at awkward situations—like what could they possibly have found at the scene to incriminate me? Unless flutes were deadly weapons now.

"To start, your flute…"

Full laugh. I couldn't help it but the absurdity of it was so humorous. Nicola slyly removed her hand from her keyboard and used one hand to nudge me under the table.

"Sorry, but that's just ridiculous. I brought my flute to play music. Music therapy is a thing. Some people find it helpful. In fact, she's the one who asked me to bring it!"

"Your flute was covered in blood, Danielle Price's fingerprints were on the end of your flute to defend herself from your attacks."

My jaw opened and I started to shake my head ever so slightly.

Nicola took over at this part. "Based on what you have said, it could have easily been the other way around. You have no way to prove who was attacking who if you have two sets of handprints on the flute."

I sat up a little taller and said a thankful prayer that I had a lawyer to help me navigate these questions.

"Do you have anything else you need to bring to my client's attention? She's been here for far too long. I'd like her to have an opportunity to eat and rest."

Officer Rossi looked at Nicola. "We have lots more. We aren't anywhere near done. We can get you some food and water if you need it but you are here for the long haul."

After putting a cheese sandwich and a water bottle in front of me, he said, "Enjoy."

He pulled out some photocopied sheets of paper and slapped them on the table. The lined yellow paper immediately registered as my therapist's notes.

"You've been seeing Dr. Price for a year, correct?"

I bobbed my head up and down slowly.

"You'll need to speak up for the record." Officer Clark barked.

"Yes."

"Look over these notes she took from your meetings. Explain to us what you see."

Without moving my head I looked over at Nicola, unsure if I should play this game or not. She gave a slight nod to tell me it was okay.

My eyes darted around the page: Easily angered, violent threats, possibly dangerous, concerned. This didn't compute. I had NEVER talked about violence towards anyone. I had never even thought about those things. How could these be her notes?

"These have to be for another client," I reasoned aloud.

"No, Ms. Frank. These are your notes. They were found in your file. The dates and times line up with sessions she had with you. We've compared them to her online scheduling system. We double checked them with the payment portal and insurance company to confirm that the sessions did in fact take place."

Since I didn't respond, one of the officers, I'm not sure who since I didn't even look up spoke.

"These notes go back for a few months."

"Months? How is that possible?"

They didn't respond but gestured towards the notes. I held the notes closer to my eyes trying to make out the blurry small print. My name and dates we'd had sessions together were in fact on the top of each page. It occurred to me that these could be a tactic used by the police to entice me to talk. The papers went all the way back to early December.

"These aren't real," I blurted out. "Even given what you said, anyone could have fabricated all this to frame me. Have you done a handwriting analysis?" Now probably wasn't the time to highlight how much I had learned from all the true crime podcasts I listen to. "I mean, like can you see if this handwriting looks like all her other notes?"

The younger officer huffed a small laugh and rolled his eyes. I turned toward my lawyer who looked blindsided by these notes.

With a more pleading tone I said again, "These can't be real. I'm telling you I've never, ever said anything violent during therapy because I don't have any violent thoughts."

"Can you please read us what it says under January?"

I really wanted to snap that they should read it themselves or better yet take it and shove it up their asses. I could clearly see through this game they were playing. They wanted me to get angry, to snap. All of this was BS.

Compliance would benefit me more though so I began to read; unsure of what I'd have to say aloud.

I cleared my throat. "Ms. Frank has spoken about jealousy in her current relationship. She has expressed that she'd key his car if she felt like he was unfaithful. I'm concerned that she could be dangerous."

"Did you key your boyfriend's car?" asked the officer.

"No, no, but it was keyed… by his ex-wife."

"Mmm…. hmm. Sure."

My voice trailed off and I pushed the notes back toward them. The buzz of other officers going about their business sounded like sirens in my ears. My hands clenched around the edge of my chair, turning my knuckles white. I had no comment so they just kept hitting me with their evidence.

"My client has zero motive to harm her therapist!"

"We disagree." The officer opened his laptop and turned it around to me. Staring back at me were screenshots of my comments regarding Dr. Price. Shit, shit, shit.

"We also found that an account tied to your email has left several extremely critical reviews of Dr. Price. Looking at the time stamp, it looks like these were posted right before she was murdered. Would you care to read those?"

"We both already know what they say."

"So, you admit you wrote those?"

"Yes, I did."

The officer began to read aloud, his tone infuriated me. "If you are looking for a second-class therapist who won't listen to a single one of your issues, you've found the right lady! Dr. Price will spend more time on her phone than listening to you. This woman is a spineless idiot who I wish I'd never wasted my time with."

He paused for me to respond. Realizing I was silent, the other officer offered, "Sounds like you were pretty angry with Dr. Price. Angry enough to kill her?"

"My God! These can't be any worse than other reviews."

"You posted these and she died shortly after. How do you think that looks? Looks like a motive to us."

For the briefest second, or what felt like it, I began to doubt myself. Maybe I had done it. How could I possibly be sure I didn't when I had no recollection?

"Have you looked into anyone else?"

Both cops couldn't hide their smirk. I could read their minds. I was the only suspect, their investigation started and stopped with me.

"Okay, I know how this looks but someone could have set me up. Have you investigated Lucas? He was also seeing Dr. Price and he has been harassing me for months now."

"Airtight alibi," was all Officer Rossi said.

I flashed back to all the things I carried with me, the things that bogged me down every day. The feeling of growing up like I was never enough, never worthy of anyone's care. The night in college. The guilt I had for Aubrey's death and the sadness it plunged into every aspect of my life today. The depression that I couldn't shake, that took days of my life. All that I carried.

But I wouldn't carry the guilt for something I didn't do.

"My client and I would like to speak privately."

We knew we were never really alone. My obsession with all things True Crime practically gave me a degree in Criminal Justice. They were always watching, always listening. I had to be very careful of what I said and did during this 'private' meeting.

The two officers turned toward each other. Without acknowledging her, they stood up and walked out of the room.

Nicola's calm but reassuring demeanor helped keep me more grounded. I stood up, using this opportunity to get out some nervous energy. I paced back and forth like a caged animal. My lawyer's voice became background noise to my own thoughts. I plunged my hands into my pockets, and one hand hit on a large cold object.

Immediately Nicola stopped mid-sentence. "What?... What?" she kept repeating.

The shock left me completely dumbfounded. I raised my hand out of my pocket, still holding onto the object. I stretched out my arm towards her, a large, shiny diamond ring between my thumb and pointer finger. Nicola's mouth was agape and then catching herself, she shut it quickly. A small gasp escaped from her.

I had been carrying my dead therapist's engagement ring in my pocket this whole time.

Chapter 37

State Correctional Facility

I ebbed and flowed between feeling hopeless and feeling determined to find the truth. It was clear that the state had a strong case against me. My lawyer, she really had a tough case to put together but she always spoke to me confidently.

All things considered, I still was able to find things to be grateful for. My mom and Talia wrote me often and visited weekly. I knew no matter what happened, there were people who cared about me. That knowledge was one of the few things that kept me going.

Of course, there was so much I resented about this place too. I missed my dog, a persistent ache in my heart to just hold him again. What a difference his cuddles would make right now! I missed my carefree dates with Christian. I missed my freedom.

If I could break out of this place right now, I'd drive straight to the shore and devour a pork roll sandwich. Or maybe Wawa—once a summer staple in our lives, I missed loading up the car with friends and hitting up the convenience store on our way to Belmar beach, grabbing hoagies, soda and chips. These small moments, at the time seemed so insignificant, but I'd do anything for them now.

The worst thing here though was my roommate. Her legal name was Carla Deitz but she made everyone call her Sunshine. It must have been one of those nicknames like calling a large man Tiny because I've never met a nastier person. I'd avoid her as much as I possibly could... which wasn't easy given that we shared a tiny cell together.

Sunshine picked up on my, 'I shouldn't be here, I'm a good girl' act real quick and instantly developed a deep dislike for me. We were all bored in here and harassing me was her form of entertainment. Considering she was five inches taller than me and had muscles the size of my head, I was completely intimidated.

Her last act was to take the sheets off my bed while I had outdoor time. She stuffed them into the toilet. I had to sleep that night on the bare mattress which smelled like the crossroads between vomit and death. For my own safety, I was too afraid to rat her out to the jail staff. Like so many things, I'd just have to let it slide.

I sat on the floor of my cell, attempting to do some stretches. Sunshine walked past and snuffed, "Look at fucking Jail Cell Barbie. Doing her morning yoga."

The woman walking next to her laughed in response. With a woman like that in your presence, you'd have to laugh at any joke she made. I ignored her as I always did. It truly didn't bother me, other than the fact that I worried her resentment towards me would escalate.

In the afternoon, we were given our mail. I'd always look forward to this because I'd often get a letter from my mom or best friend. My life had changed so much in such a short time. One moment, I had been excited about trips with my boyfriend, now all I had to look forward to was a few letters a week. I used to worry about oversleeping and not having enough time to make my morning coffee run before work. Now, I was worried if I looked at my roommate wrong, I'd end up hanging by my bedsheets.

I ran my fingers through my hair and clumps of it were intertwined on my fingers. My clothes were fitting more loosely. I couldn't be sure but I must have lost about twenty pounds. Looking at my reflection in the mirror, my skin was dull.

Thinking of Christian caused my heart to ache. We weren't together for a very long time but our chemistry was amazing. I thought it would have blossomed into a deep love, possibly a long-term relationship. I'd be lying if I didn't admit that I had daydreamed about us possibly getting married.

There were times when I thought we'd save each other from the traumas we had. Now I sat alone, wondering where he was and what he was up to. Maybe he moved on and was dating again. Maybe he didn't even think about me, our time together just a blip in his timeline. Maybe he was even back with his wife.

My mind stopped wandering when the guard came by my cell and handed me three envelopes.

He had none for Sunshine. "Sorry," he said gruffly to her. She rolled her eyes at him and said nothing.

I took the envelopes and tried to huddle in the back corner of my bottom bunk, hiding away from her.

The return addresses were from my mom, Talia and an unmarked one. Curiosity got the best of me and I flipped over the back of the envelope to open it. Before I could start to tear the paper, Sunshine ripped it from my hands. She gave me a taunting smile.

She slowly opened it while starring at me. It was a game to her and I didn't want to be a part of it. My reaction was to keep a stone face and still body. She'd give me back the envelope once she got bored.

Once it was opened, she scrunched her face and then took the paper to her nose. A deep loud cackle came from my cellmate as my own confusion grew. "You're getting fucking scented letters in the mail, Barbie?" She threw her head back and gave a maniacal laugh. "You are too fucking much!"

She tossed me the envelope and letter but they fell to the ground in front of me. I scrambled to reach for it and opened the letter. The unmistakable scent of lavender filled my nose, taking me back to Dr. Price's office.

I opened the letter, which simply had typed: Say more.

Chapter 38

With the letter gripped in my hands, I read it over and over again. Two words. How could two words hold so much mystery? As those two words bounced around in my head, my cellmate looked over at the expression stained on my face and couldn't resist the temptation to mock me.

"Christ, you look like you saw a fucking ghost."

"I think I did," I muttered under my breath.

Later in the day, it was time for visitations. I was pretty sure I'd get a visitor today and I was jittery with excitement. Working with the resources I had, I tried my best to look nice. I smoothed out my hair using my fingers and then twisted it into a bun. When I looked in the mirror, I didn't like what I saw. My mind became flooded with negative thoughts as I berated myself—my skin was too pale, my face gaunt, my hair thinning. My eyes stung with hot tears as I continued to glare at myself with disdain.

The guard led me into the room, and sitting at the table was both my mother and Talia. They both stood and embraced me in an awkward three-person hug. The feeling of my mother's body against mine was something I had taken for granted but in this moment, it made me feel like I was going to be okay. Once we sat down, we settled into the normal rhythm where I asked the same set of questions.

"How are you? How's Winston? Give him cuddles for me. How's work? What are your plans for the weekend?"

I listened to their reports of daily life. Snapshots from the outside. They didn't realize how special running to the grocery store, a chore I used to dread, would be for me right now. I envied their freedom.

Despite the sameness of each visit, I did love hearing about what they were up to. It gave me a few moments of feeling normal, as if we were in a coffee shop talking. If the coffee shop was bleak as hell and smelled of mold.

After we went through that, I pulled out the letter. Both Talia and my mother looked at it, unsure how to react. They leaned in together looking the short letter over.

"What's it mean?" I tilted my head to Talia.

"It's from Lucas. It's something our therapist would say to us. He's telling me to confess."

Talia shook her head.

Shots of anger pulsed through me. "When will you stop defending this asshole?"

Talia looked around to see if others were starting to stare at us. She reached for the envelope and inspected it.

She lowered her voice in an effort to calm me. "Isabella, Lucas has been in Puerto Rico for the past two weeks. He couldn't have hurt Dr. Price and he couldn't have mailed this letter."

I took back the envelope, just now noticing the stamp that read "Burlington, VT". As soon as she stopped speaking, she looked away, a veil of sadness over her face.

I couldn't place where the emotion was coming from. Was she lying to cover for him and feeling guilty about it? Or was Lucas causing her pain? Had he physically, verbally or mentally hurt her? Maybe she just missed him while he was away. I just couldn't read her when it came to Lucas.

"Well maybe..." I started to protest and then realized I couldn't come up with an explanation. Talia, who must have had the patience of a saint, put her hand on mine.

"I know it's impossible to see it now, but I promise you it's going to be okay," she reassured. "Your mom and I are going to do everything to have the truth come out. We know you are innocent. But, Isabella, the answer isn't him. Lucas has his problems but he absolutely didn't do it."

I nodded and lowered my head.

Tears welled in my eyes as I tried hard to keep them back. Big tears smacked the table and splattered like little explosions as they hit the hard surface. Neither woman said anything, letting me have my moment to let this all wash over me. My mother came closer to me and rubbed my back while I continued to cry.

Lucas was my only hope.

Now I was hopeless.

Chapter 39

Later that night, I laid in my bed unable to fall asleep. I tossed and turned as quietly as possible. The mattress was stiff and thin with the springs often jabbing me in the back. It probably held as many germs as a public toilet. Insomnia had become a regular problem. Thoughts toiled through my mind and never relented enough to allow me to rest.

The letter still consumed me and I thought my next plan of action would be to talk to my lawyer about it. If Lucas wasn't a possible suspect, we'd have to figure out who else would have a motive to hurt me and to hurt Dr. Price.

Hurt Dr. Price.

I still allowed my mind to play tricks on me as I couldn't bring myself to say what actually happened to her.

I began to get letters pretty frequently. At first, they were all the same. They reeked of lavender and simply said: Say more.

After a week, they started to shift. Each letter more disturbing than the last. All were postmarked from southern Vermont.

Mentally, I flipped through every yearbook, every staff meeting, every casual interaction. I couldn't think of a single person who had relocated from here to Vermont. It had always been on my list of places to visit. The photos transported you to a cozy winter retreat decorated with dark woods and red flannels, sipping a steaming hot coffee by the fire, seeing snowcapped mountains out your window. I had never made it there and now likely never would.

I began to play back conversations of people who had mentioned vacationing there. Several people posted about it over the years- smiling faces with beautiful backgrounds. Of course, Vermont was a stunning landscape and only a five-hour getaway from Central New Jersey. None of those people who talked about weekends skiing or summers hiking there had any issues with me… that I could think of at least.

The letters were a dead end at this point.

Chapter 40

Nicola was set to visit with me today at 2:00 pm. I watched each minute pass by which made time go excruciatingly slow. When the time finally arrived, I was brought to a bare room where we could discuss my situation. I tossed the pile of letters on the table. She placed her black briefcase beside her as she sat across from me. I thought to myself cynically how ridiculous she looked in a pants suit and nice flats while in this disgusting room. Her floral perfume wafted through the smell of the body odor of two-hundred and fifty women who no longer gave a shit about impressing anyone.

My lawyer looked at me and asked, "What's all this?"

"Read them," I snapped. I realized I was being a bitch but that realization did nothing to curb my attitude.

She slowly opened each letter and read them. The confusion was written all over her face. "I don't understand. Do these have meaning to you?"

"If they did, don't you think I'd tell you." I rolled my eyes.

Nicola took in a breath before responding. Her patience with me was waning. She spoke softly to me as if I was a small child. "I know you are hurting, angry, frustrated, sad. You are justified in feeling those things because you are in a really awful situation. But we have to work as a team."

I propped my elbows on the table and cradled my face with my hands. Sitting there, I just bawled. Every emotion I had been bottling up came to the surface like an erupting volcano. My sobs were loud and uncontrollable. Nicola sat across from me silently for a while, letting me work through my emotions.

After several minutes she coaxed, "Let's try to figure this all out. We aren't going to make any progress if we continue like this."

I was itching to argue with her. "I don't know what it all means and I feel like you aren't helping," I snapped.

And with that, I could tell she was done. "Cut the shit, Isabella. You want to screw yourself over? Does that seem logical to you? Knock it off and help me to help you."

She was right. I knew it and had to swallow my pride and apologize.

After I calmed down, I said, "I'm sorry. I know you are here to help but I'm just so, so frustrated. I don't know what these mean but I do know it has some link to Danielle Price. She used to say that line a lot in our sessions. I feel like someone is taunting me for hurting both of us but pinning it on me. I was sure it was Lucas but that's seems to be a dead end."

"How so?"

"Talia told me he was in Puerto Rico and has been for a while now."

"I'll look into that to confirm."

She took out her writing tablet and began to jot down ideas on how to figure out this mystery. She wrote:

1. Check flight records for Lucas Marin.
2. Investigate any personal links between Isabella and someone in Burlington, VT and surrounding areas.
3. Contact post office, have envelopes and letters fingerprinted.

She was action oriented and seeing her list of action items made me feel hopeful that one of these might lead somewhere.

The police visited me later that day. It was two new cops I hadn't met yet. They told me their names but I didn't listen. We sat at a rectangular table and while I knew I needed to focus, all I could think about was the damp smell in the room. It was overbearing.

"We got a warrant to search your house."

I wasn't worried, there was zero evidence that I had anything to do with this, nothing to show I had a motive. Then one of the officers pushed a photo toward me, it was of my refrigerator in my kitchen. My jaw went slack as I sat staring at a fridge in a kitchen that I recognized as mine, except it wasn't how I had left it the last time I was home.

This cream-colored fridge, which had bite marks on the handle from Winston, was covered in photos. The officers then produced the full-size photos, each in a clear plastic container. There were ten photos, each of Christian with a woman next to him, but the woman was completely marked up with black sharpie.

"Ms. Frank, we've given you lots of opportunities to come clean about what really happened to Danielle Price. Every opportunity you've lied to us. I think it's time you confess."

They thought they were ready to wrap this up but I was like twenty steps behind them. "I'm sorry—I've never seen these photos."

"They were on your fridge. They have your fingerprints on them."

"That's impossible," I stammered. "These photos… I don't understand."

"Sure, but take a close look at them. Who is the guy?"

"That's my boy… that's my… we were dating."

"What is his name, Ms. Frank?"

"His name is Christian Sandoval."

"And who is the woman?"

The woman had so much marker over her that it was impossible to tell. I told them this and of course they didn't believe me.

"Who was shown in this photo before you crossed it out?"

"I didn't have these photos, I didn't mark them up, and I didn't hang them on my fridge so as much as I'd love to help you, I can't," I said defiantly.

"Have it your way. I'll help you figure it out."

The officer took one of the photos out of the plastic bag. Beside him he took out a white cotton ball and some Lysol. He sprayed the cotton ball and gently rubbed it back and forth over the black sharpie. Slowly the marker dissolved, like my heart, because there standing next to Christian was Dr. Danielle Price.

Chapter 41

~~────────────~~

"So now what do you have to say?" The officer sounded so cocky like he was enjoying taunting me.

Questions flooded my mind but I wasn't sure how to respond to the officers. After looking at the picture, I began to examine the others more closely. The photos showed Christian, smiling happily next to Dr. Price. In a few of them, they stood closely together. Some of the photos, the ones he appeared a bit older, you could tell the smile was forced, because his eyes weren't smiling too. In those forced smile photos, they had more distance between them.

"My boyfriend was also seeing my therapist?" Jesus what was even happening right now? "He told me he didn't like therapists. He was against therapy."

Both officers' faces immediately changed and I could tell I had said something stupid.

"That isn't his therapist. That is his wife."

"His..." The room started to blur and I felt like I might faint. I gripped the edge of the table with both hands to steady myself. "His... his..." I repeated almost inaudibly.

"Danielle Price Sandoval is the wife of Christian Sandoval the man who had been seeing you on the side for several months. They had been married for ten years until we suspect you murdered her out of jealousy. It's why you did this; and keyed his car to get his attention and tried to pin it on her. You found out she was pregnant and lost it, worried he was going to run back to her. You couldn't let that happen, could you? So, you stopped them from reconnecting by taking her life."

I stood up from the table as the room spun like I was on the teacups ride. So many emotions flowed through my body that I wasn't even sure I had an ounce of control over what I was doing. I felt overwhelmingly nauseous and I wasn't sure if I was going to vomit right there in front of everyone. "I need to speak to my lawyer immediately."

I was escorted back to my cell, where only my thoughts were there to torture me. Each moment I had with Christian played in my mind. That's when something clicked. I had told Christian about how Dr. Price always told me to 'say more'.

The letters were from Vermont, a place Christian had last asked me to go with him... before I couldn't go anywhere. Christian had been in my apartment several times so maybe he stole one of my spare keys and made a copy. Using that key, he could have planted things in my apartment. And of course, there was the fact that as soon as I landed here in jail, I never heard a word from him again.

At this point, I had convinced myself that Christian was involved. My ex-boyfriend was a murderer. The thought disgusted me. Someone I cared for could do this to me and I never even had a clue. I needed to have Nicola help me make this case. Both anger, confusion and heartbreak consumed me. I had been falling in love with this man, and he had betrayed me and used me as if I was a pawn in a game.

Chapter 42

Another visitation day rolled around and I had so much I wanted to tell my mother. When I was escorted to her table, she stood and reached out to stroke my arm. Immediately I got choked up as tears hovered in the corner of my eyes. I didn't want to cry so I rapidly blinked them away.

She handed me a few photos of Winston. Each picture was more adorable than the next. I knew I'd hang these up near my bed when I got back to my room. I liked to call it a room rather than a cell. It was slightly less depressing.

We sat down across from each other. I began to tell her the story of everything.

"He used me, mom."

As I recounted it, each element stung. The photos in my apartment, the betrayal by my boyfriend and all the evidence the police had against me. As I told this story, I noticed my mother ringing her hands.

"Bella..." she said cautiously.

"What? What is it?"

She gulped before speaking. "I just want you to know, I only did this because I care about you."

"Yes…" I encouraged her.

"I'm sorry… please don't be mad. After our session, Dr. Price asked me to stay."

"Yeah, I know."

"Well… we had both been very concerned about your mental health. You seemed to be spiraling into such a depression—it was terrifying for me to watch and not be able to do anything to help you. Dr. Price asked me if I would provide her with a key to your apartment because we were both concerned… about you possibly self-harming."

"She had a key to my apartment? How could you!" I slammed my fist onto the table. "Who knows what type of lunatics she was working with. Anyone of them could have stolen that key and entered my apartment. Maybe that is how Christian got the key to my house."

"Please try to understand my sweet girl," my mother said, trying unsuccessfully to pacify me. She reached out her hand to touch me and I pulled away. "She told me you were at risk of self-harming or I think she called it 'unaliving' yourself. I was completely panicked. You are my world and I just wanted to do whatever it would take to keep you safe. She told me that having access would let her be able to get into your place quickly to help you if you weren't responding during one of your… low points."

"Mother, this is unforgivable." I stood to leave as the guards began to approach us when I heard her voice crack.

"I... I just didn't want to lose you."

She was ringing her hands again, the sign I always recognized when she was overwhelmed with any negative emotion.

Seeing the sheer panic in her face, even thinking back to that moment, I did start to calm down. She just wanted to do what was best for me. I suppose she and Dr. Price were just trying to protect me and I have to admit, that I probably would have done the same to protect my own child.

I was starting to get a clearer vision of what I thought might have happened. Dr. Price had the key to my apartment for safety reasons. Christian stole that key and set me up for her murder. All that talk of trying to get a divorce had been a ruse, a con.

Though he treated me like his girlfriend, I was a pawn in order to rid himself of his unhappy marriage.

It wouldn't be the first time a man snapped after hearing his wife was pregnant and took her life. I was convinced that this is what had to have happened, but thinking of the way Christian looked at me, so tenderly, made it hard to reconcile those two versions of him.

My mind began to play a movie of Christian getting access to Danielle's life insurance. Then him buying a luxury car. Finally, him laying on a tropical island at a five-star resort. Probably with someone prettier than me, and definitely a lot less screwed up.

Despite this image being so vivid, it was hard to wrap my mind around how I could have been tricked. After the many deep conversations we had, hours in each other's arms and loving kisses, I really believed he cared for me.

"Please sit," my mother said, snapping me back into reality and away from my swirling and conflicting thoughts.

I sat down next to her and put my head on her shoulder. "I'm sorry I put you through that."

"Bella, never, never apologize for that." She kissed my forehead.

Despite the fact that Christian and I were out of contact and had been for a long time now, I needed a moment to grieve this once blossoming relationship. We had bonded so well and it was all fake. I didn't understand how to process all the time we had spent together that felt so real, so genuine. How would I trust anyone ever again?

Chapter 43

"Shut the fuck up!" Sunshine called down to me in the middle of the night.

I was sobbing uncontrollably in my bed. The tears came hard and fast and soon I was hyperventilating. It felt like someone was sticking their hand down my throat and yanking my breath out of me. I cupped my hands over my mouth to act as a bag, hoping it would slow my strong, audible breathing.

"Jailhouse Barbie, are you fucking dying down there?" she barked as she kicked the flimsy bed frame, shaking us both.

I wasn't trying to ignore her but I couldn't speak in that moment. I heard her start to jump onto the ladder and descend to where I was. I braced myself for her wrath.

She looked at me and could see the panic in my eyes. I continued to labor with my breathing as loud gasps escaped me. My tears continued through it all. Sunshine looked at me considering what to do. I assumed she was considering if she should punch me or stuff my head in the toilet. To be fair, both of those solutions would have probably stopped my hyperventilation.

For whatever reason, she sat next to me on the bed.

"Knock it off bitch," she said softly. "Shit, you can't die. They will think I did it. It'll all be okay."

My whole life had become so absurd I couldn't help but laugh. Laughing had become so infrequent that it rolled out of me like a boulder down a hill. There was no stopping it.

She side-eyed me. "You're crazy."

As my breathing started to normalize, I nodded back at her and when I could finally speak, I said, "I know. Thanks for sitting with me."

"Don't mention it—literally."

With that, she crawled back up to her bed and soon we were both lightly snoring, the sound of the guards pacing back and forth our lullaby.

The next morning, when I crawled out of bed, I wasn't sure how to greet my roommate. Were we friendly now? Or was that just a moment of kindness that I'd never get again?

While trying to process this, she kicked my leg but there wasn't much energy to it.

"You know, if you didn't do it, the truth's gonna come out. Sometimes people make it out of here."

"Yeah, maybe. Right now, they've thrown more at me than I think I can work out. How about you? You trying to get out too?"

"Hell no. I definitely deserve to be here," she said with a demonic laugh. I decided I was better off not knowing why she was here and left it at that.

"Has anyone gotten out after a conviction?"

"Here? Not that I know of. Justice system is shit. Some people have gotten DNA proving they were innocent and they still stay locked up. But maybe it is different for you—like someone is trying to tell you something, with all those letters, right? They gonna help you, Barbie. You just gotta figure out what they are trying to tell you."

I thought about the letters. So simple. 'Say more'.

Was it a threat like I assumed? Or was it a message, a hint? I took out a piece of paper and wrote down what still needed answering:

Had Christian and Danielle filed for divorce or started those proceedings in any way?

Who knew about Danielle's line of 'say more'?

Did any of her clients have a grudge against her?

Did Christian know I was seeing Danielle?

What message was the sender of these letters trying to tell me?

Who would want to help me but was afraid of getting involved?

The most important question—After I had all the answers, would it make any difference?

Chapter 44

Nicola called me the next day. My hand, slightly trembling, was gripped around the black phone handle as I huddled in the small booth.

"Isabella? Can you hear me?" she said over the static.

"Yeah. What did you find?" I asked eagerly.

"Christian Sandoval filed for divorce from his wife Danielle Price Sandoval over a year before her death. They did not have children, which can significantly complicate a divorce. However, they had accumulated significant wealth and property since their marriage. This has caused it to take much longer than the standard divorce time frame. Also, there is a record of legal separation for two years before he filed for divorce."

My heart was pounding in my chest so hard it was visible through my shirt. I felt unwell and was worried I might faint from this news. I raised my palm to my forehead and began rubbing it. Christian telling the truth added some questions to my hypothesis. Everything was changing so fast that I felt like my theories were morphing day to day.

"And Isabella…" She took a long pause. All I could hear was static and I was worried we got disconnected.

"Yes?"

"I made contact with Mr. Sandoval."

I felt like I had been punched in the gut. The wind had been taken out of me. I almost didn't even want to hear what he had to say. My world was so upside down that I didn't think I could handle anything—good, bad, or in between. In my confusion, I just stayed silent waiting for her to tell me whatever he had to say.

"Due to the current circumstance, his lawyer has advised him not to make any formal contact with you as it could affect your case. He asked me to pass along a message. He said he misses you and will reach out as soon as he is allowed to."

A minute went by without me saying anything.

"Are you still there?"

My voice cracked as I said, "Yeah." I pushed away the tears even though she couldn't see them.

"Do you have anything you'd like me to pass along to him?"

Several beats went by and all I could get out was, "No, thank you."

With that, I said goodbye and hung up the phone, my whole body shaking.

The quivering sensation brought me back to that night in college. I felt like I was in that moment again. I couldn't see anything but I could feel things. There were hands on my breasts, squeezing hard. Several hands running up and down my legs, going between my thighs but over my pants. There was a body laying on top of me, the pressure of their weight making it hard to breathe. Their body rocking back and forth on top of mine giving me the sensation of being on a boat tossed around in the ocean.

Sounds were coming back too. Laugher. So loud. They drunkenly laughed at me—at what they could do to me. They called out the names of other boys, calling them to join in. More hands roamed all over me. Then the sounds changed. Anger. Yelling. GET THE FUCK OFF HER. And then the powerful sound of a fist making contact with bone. A crack.

When the image was gone, I sucked in a deep breath, as if I had been deprived of air that whole time.

Later when I was just left with my thoughts, I wondered... if I could bring myself back to that moment, to those feelings, to those sounds... maybe I could recall something from that night that took Dr. Price and brought me here.

Chapter 45

Being escorted by jail guards to the family meeting room always made me sarcastically chuckle. At this point I couldn't be more than 115 pounds at 5 foot 3 inches and not a strong muscle in my body. I wasn't really a risk to anyone around me. Hell, I wasn't even a threat to a jar of pickles. I couldn't believe that anyone would think I'd need two guards to escort me. Although based on what they are excusing me of doing, they clearly thought I was diabolical. The idea that I'd hurt someone, let alone kill them was unfathomable.

The guards took me to the room. I scanned the room but didn't see my normal visitors. Then my eyes landed on him and I was frozen solid. There at the table, sitting alone and nervously tapping on the table, was Lucas.

He looked better than before, a little more put together. I became like a caged animal and turned my back trying to scramble to get out. The guards, not understanding that I was reacting in fear, thought I might be trying to escape. They each wrapped their thick hands around my arm to keep me in place. My legs moved frantically but I made no progress toward. The guards not realizing their own strength, their grip quickly began to hurt.

"You are hurting me," I screamed. "Please let me go."

I wanted to make sure that he wasn't coming towards me so I glanced over my shoulder. Lucas stood at the table frozen like a deer in headlights. As we locked eyes, he held up both hands in a surrendering pose.

Seeing how alarmed he was, made me calm down. I stopped scrambling and tried to turn, letting the guards know I wasn't going anywhere. They looked at each other and nodded, slowly releasing the pressure on my arms, just to make sure I was keeping my word. The pressure from their grip ached even after they let go and I instinctively began rubbing the area. I started to walk timidly towards Lucas, assessing with each step if I still felt like this was a wise choice.

Lucas slid back into the chair and I sat across from him. I was unsure what to say or even what tone to take with him, so I waited for him to speak first. We sat there letting the silence ease us into our first real conversation since before Aubrey's death.

He continued to tap his fingers on the table and though the sound wasn't that loud, it felt like a heartbeat in my ear. Understandably, I felt ill at ease with him and my stomach clenched. He had been harassing me for months. Why was he here? And why did I want to hear what he had to say so badly?

"How's Talia?" he asked me, as he took off his ball cap, placing it on the table.

I glared at him questioningly. "Why don't you know how Talia is?" My voice was full of disdain for this man.

He glanced down at his hands. "We haven't spoken since I went to Puerto Rico."

"Call her Lucas. She needs you."

I still didn't approve of their relationship but she sure as hell shouldn't be ghosted during this traumatic time in her life. She needed closure on a whole hell of a lot of things and shouldn't be adding this to the list. The young hurt boy across from me sighed deeply and told me he would reach out to her.

"You look tan. What were you doing there?"

"I have family there. But mostly just escaping everything."

"Escaping." I chuckled. "I'd say that sounds nice, but don't want to give anyone the wrong idea or they'd probably have a guard on me 24/7."

He smirked at me but said nothing at first.

"I needed to get away from here because I couldn't recognize myself anymore. I can't even stand to be around me most days, does that make sense?"

"Yeah, yeah, I definitely get that. Are you feeling any better?"

He paused for a while, taking in a deep breathe. "Maybe a little. I don't even know." He forced a smile that only showed sadness.

We let silence creep in and it became awkward. Though I didn't have much else to do with my day other than sit right here at this table, I was tired of beating around the bush.

"Why are you here, Lucas?" I blurted out.

"I'm sorry," he said and just left it at that. If he came for peace, I thought I could at least attempt to be civil.

"I'm sorry, too," I replied, not exactly clear about what aspects we were apologizing for.

He lowered his head and I could see the corners of his lips curl up in a small smile. "You don't have anything to apologize for. I came here because… I'm apologizing for the way I went about trying to warn you."

This made no sense to me. "Warn me?" I asked slowly. "What do you mean?"

"I left the note on your door, tried having your co-worker pass along the message and tried calling you, too."

"You have no idea how much fear I lived because of you." I kept my voice low so we wouldn't get in trouble but tried to put as much anger as one could in a low whisper.

"What about all those times you were stalking me?"

Lucas's response was not what I expected. He looked genuinely surprised.

"Stalking? I was trying to keep an eye on you." His voice, his facial expression. There was something about it—it felt genuine. Talking here face to face, I started to feel differently towards him. I think I believed what he was saying.

"I know I went about it all wrong. I know that now at least. That's why I am here… to apologize for scaring you. I really was fucked in the head and every step I took was just handled like shit. I'm sorry for that and the way I made you feel."

"So, if you weren't harassing me. Tell me this: The note you left, the one that said, 'Beware Of Her'… what the hell type of warning were you leaving by letting my neighbors think I was dangerous?"

"Wait… what?" He laughed sardonically. "Isabella, I wasn't warning them about you. I was warning you about Dr. Price."

Chapter 46

I sat back in my cell trying to make sense of everything that had come to light in the past few days. Lucas told me that Dr. Price knew I was dating her husband and was both heartbroken at her failing marriage and furious at me for making it final. Lucas recounted the time he came into my car, admitted it was borderline crazy, which he apologized for, blaming it on a moment of insanity. He said after the incident she brought him into her office and had him sitting with her for nearly an hour. Dr. Price thought she had found the perfect person to manipulate. She tried to calm him down and as she did, she kept throwing out breadcrumbs to see if he would take the bait.

Lucas became alarmed with the questioning when she started to ask him to elaborate on his anger.

"So, what exactly would you like to do to her?" she had asked him.

"It was like she was egging me on to do worse, instead of see what I had done wrong," he told me.

He felt her demeanor was strange and though he did harbor a lot of anger toward me, he began to feel uncomfortable. He said she got up, and sat right next to him, running her fingers along his arm, asking if they might make a good team.

"I asked her what she meant," Lucas had recounted. He said she smiled at him seductively.

"I think you know what I mean," she had said to him as she moved from running her fingers up his arm to running her hands onto his chest.

"The rage in her eyes struck a chord of fear in me like I've never felt before. She never said it directly but she kept talking about this team we would be. How we could seek revenge together. She was very persuasive. I think she wanted me to hurt you, like follow through on my lapse of insanity in your car. Instead of dousing the flames of anger, she was stoking them—right there in her office. I don't know how far she would have taken it but she wanted you to hurt like she did—maybe even die for it."

I recalled everything he said to me in that room. I kept repeating that in my mind laying on the side of my paper-thin mattress. Lucas recounted to me how, in the moment, he agreed to help her, knowing he wouldn't hurt me but would try to prevent her from doing whatever it was that she planned.

"Why Lucas? Why did you do all this when you hated me so much?" I had said to him.

"If something happened to you, Talia would never be the same. I didn't save Aubrey, but I could save Talia from more grief."

Knowing this, Lucas became determined to stop Dr. Price. He met with her several times, trying to find out her intentions, her plans. And then he created his own plan.

I flipped on the mattress, turning my conversation over and over like a movie projected in my mind. Each of the wires beneath it was poking into my back but, in that moment, I didn't care. My heart began to pound so hard that I could feel my blood pulse through my veins. I bolted up like a flash of lighting.

Through the darkness of the jail, my yell reverberated through the empty hallway.

"That bitch did it to herself!"

Chapter 47

~~―――――――――――~~

I picked up one of the letters and deeply inhaled the scent of lavender. Suddenly, the world became black and I was back in the moment. I'm laying on the floor. There are footsteps around me, going back and forth. I hear the sound of something being dragged. The sound of metal on bone. I feel coldness around me. Someone is shouting at me.

"He's mine!" is whispered loudly in my ear and then, THUNK!

The moment slips away and I am back in my own world, confused.

"Fuck! Please, please let me use the phone," I screamed at the woman at the first phone booth I saw. When she looked at me, I could see she had a tear drop tattoo that clearly showed she wasn't to be messed with. These tattoos can stand for several things but can often be a sign that you've taken someone's life.

All the other phones were taken and I desperately needed to speak to my lawyer. I paced up and down the corridor, waiting for a phone to become free. As soon as I heard the word 'bye', I dashed in the direction of the voice and slipped in as soon as it was unoccupied. Frantically, I dialed Nicola and I was relieved that she picked up on the second ring.

Breathlessly I told her everything I had learned in the last several hours and all my speculations. I waited for her reaction, praying she was as convinced as I was.

"You understand what you are trying to tell me is extremely far-fetched, and I give it about zero chance that the police will investigate this. In fact, it makes no sense. Isabella, they found the body of Danielle Price. How can we ask them to look into her masterminding this fantasy you created? I'm not trying to be unkind… but we need to be realistic. It is not happening," Nicola said.

I could tell she was really, really trying to restrain herself. It was clear that she thought I was in a state of mania.

"Please, just look into it. Talk to Lucas. Talk to Christian. I swear once you hear it from them, you will look at this differently. Please, Nicola. Please."

Nicola responded to me sympathetically. "I'm not a private investigator."

Going into this conversation I was holding myself high, confident that I knew what happened. However, if I couldn't convince anyone, the whole revelation was pointless. My shoulders began to slouch and I slipped down in the metal chair just now feeling its coldness on my skin.

"I'll look into getting a P.I."

"Thank you! Thank you! Thank you!" I was cautiously optimistic but Nicola's voice was devoid of any emotion. I doubted I would hear back on it.

Chapter 48

May 2024

The morning air was cool and I didn't have on nearly enough clothing to keep warm. Since the weather wasn't ideal, there weren't many people outdoors and the quiet helped me to focus. The large fluffy clouds above moved slowly through the bright blue sky. I watched them move as I thought about all the facts I had and the speculations I held.

I paced in the outdoor space, using the time and the fresh air to help me sort through all that I had learned. Danielle's body had been found, but that didn't mean she couldn't have harmed me, set the stage and then died by suicide, making it look like murder.

She was an extremely smart woman so she had the intelligence to pull this off. But was she that conniving? That evil? Was it possible that the police hadn't even looked into other possibilities due to the fact that Danielle had set the stage so well? I was well aware that it looked like an open and shut case.

Then there was the fact that she was pregnant. No matter how much she wanted revenge on me, would she also take her unborn child with her in the process? I just couldn't see that happening. Also—was Christian the father? I pushed that out of my mind for now as it would unleash a whole plethora of other questions, not to mention negative emotions. I knew I was on to something but there is definitely a part here that I was missing.

The next day, Nicola called me and I was dreading this conversation as I picked up the receiver. My fate hung on this phone call. I was sure she'd find whatever evidence fit her narrative. My theory on what happened was too far-fetched for even the person defending me to buy it. And if I didn't have her on my side, I had no one.

"So, I don't have any good news for you yet."

Of course, I thought.

"Why are you calling then?" I whined like a middle school teenager. My emotions were all over the place as if I was back in that time period of my life.

"I'm calling because Christian sent me a message to give to you. He asked me to pass along the message that he would like to know if he can come meet with you."

I wasn't at all prepared for this. Why now? After all this time apart and we've had no contact, why would he want to see me now? I felt all thoughts slip from my mind. Then a warmth, a tingly feeling wrapped around me. I had been so isolated and the idea of a friend, any friend, was a huge relief.

"Yes! Yes, please have him reach out," I said enthusiastically. If anything, it would be good to have another person to connect with even if it did come with a mixed bag of emotions.

Before she hung up, she told me she was still waiting to hear back from a few private investigators and would call me as soon as she had a contract.

"Thank you for trying," I said.

That was all I could ask for in this moment and if she was trying, there was still hope that the truth could come out… and maybe I could get out of here one day.

After hanging up, I went back to my cell and tried to envision what seeing Christian again would be like. Both nervous and excited, I was looking forward to the next visitation day.

Chapter 49

Finally, the day came, and as the guards walked me into the room, I paused seeing him. I tried to gauge his reaction to me so I knew how to mirror his emotion. When his eyes met mine, he gave me a huge sympathetic smile. He stepped forward towards me and Christian and I embraced briefly. He pulled away to look at me.

"I'm so sorry… for everything, Isabella. For you being here, for me being out of contact, for not being there to help you."

I let him explain why he had been out of contact for so long. His lawyer strongly suggested that we stay out of touch so it didn't appear as if we had plotted this together. It was for both of our benefits, he explained. His demeanor, his voice all felt genuine to me.

"I understand," I said solemnly.

In that moment, I contemplated sharing with Christian that I somehow felt that Danielle was involved in her own death. It was illogical and I decided to hold back. I couldn't risk pushing him away at this point or having him think I had gone crazy. Having Christian in my life, even in this limited capacity was worth a whole hell of a lot to me right now.

I locked my eyes on his. "I didn't do this," I said.

"God, I know that, Isa," he replied.

"No one else seems to feel that way." I looked down at my hands, feeling defeated. Then I looked back up at him. "What made you come now?"

"I was told not to come."

"Okay—but why did you come now?"

"I knew you couldn't have had anything to do with this. I listened to my lawyers advise but started digging. I don't want to get your hopes up. But I think I might have learned something that could—"

The guards abruptly told everyone that their time was up.

"I'll write to you. It was good to see you," he said, as he reached for my hand and gave it a little squeeze.

I wished for more, so much more. A small kiss would be heaven. My mind played images of him wrapping his arms around me and kissing me passionately. All I had now were fantasies. Our life together as a normal, happy couple was over.

After seeing him, I recalled our carefree days together and I wanted to reach through time and space and bring myself back to them. The memories came fast like little lights blinking in the distance. I began to feel myself slipping away again. The familiar feeling returned, my body heavy, my mind devoid of thought.

When I returned to the cell, I felt empty. Like a small child, I crawled to the corner of my bed and wrapped my arms around my knees. I rocked back and forth slowly until finally I fell asleep.

Several days later, I got a letter and I hoped that it was from Christian. My heart did small palpitations as I ran my finger along the envelope to open it. I pulled out the white printer paper and unfolded it.

I flipped through the pages. Each was a print out from a dating site. Each woman was listed as 5 foot 7 inches, longer dark blonde hair, brown eyes, fair skin. They all looked extremely similar. One of them had a small baby bump. And they all looked like Danielle Price.

The last page just said—These were on her internet search history.

Another piece clicked into place.

I took out an envelope and paper. I began to write quickly with quaking hands:

'Find a way to get back with her.'

That's all I wrote. I hoped he would know what it meant.

Chapter 50

2 months later

The smell of coffee hit me as I walked through the door. The small coffee shop was pretty crowded and I was just getting used to being around people again. Momentarily, I thought of turning around and leaving. Then I told myself I needed to start adjusting to regular life again. I put on my bulky noise canceling headphones after ordering, hoping the lack of noise would help me retreat into myself. While I was thankful for my freedom, it also terrified me.

I pulled out a card I bought on the way here. I scribbled a note to Carla, while I'd probably not be able to bring myself to visit for a long time, maybe ever, I thought I could brighten her day keeping in touch with her. With pen in hand, I wrote a heartfelt thank you to the woman who caused me a lot of stress but pulled me through my darkest days. As corny as it was, I thought to myself that the name Sunshine wasn't such a bad nickname for her after all.

My iPad was propped on the table and I felt like I was finally ready to read the news articles. I opened the browser and went to the news site:

Woman Believed to Be Dead Resurfaces After Honey Trap

Danielle Price, who was thought to be deceased, has been located living under an assumed identity.

This story started off while Dr. Price was a therapist to a wayward young lady, who has declined to comment but has been identified as Isabella Frank. The duo had a professional working relationship for about a year. During one of their sessions, Dr. Price discovered that the young woman was dating her estranged husband. The husband, Christian Sandoval, was also unaware of this connection.

Dr. Price began to exhibit increasingly erratic behavior as she plotted to use her position to split the two lovebirds. She attempted to use their sessions to convince Ms. Frank to leave the relationship. When that had mixed results, she resorted to more extreme measures. Dr. Price began to secretly harass Ms. Frank, including breaking into her apartment several times to cause psychological distress.

Dr. Price had called her husband before the murder to say she was pregnant with his child, which he knew was impossible. She even went as far as trying to lure one of her patients into assisting with her plan.

This patient, Lucas Marino, chose to speak to the Hamilton Gazette.

"Dr. Price used me when I was at my lowest point. She tried to manipulate me into hurting another person, someone I have known for years. She's completely crazy." The young man added after a pause, "I hope she never gets out."

According to the parents of Price's victim, Denise Yarrow had been estranged from the family for many years.

"Unfortunately, our Denise took a bad path many, many years ago. She's been addicted to drugs for over a decade and we had cut her off when she began stealing from family members," said her mother, through tears and sniffles.

Dr. Price began scouring internet dating sites for those who closely resembled her. When she located a near look alike, she began to catfish the woman, pretending to be a potential suitor. After weeks of talking, the victim was lured to Dr. Price's office where she was drugged and held in her office closet.

She then drugged her unsuspecting patient as well. With both women incapacitated, she was able to set out on her evil plan. She used the young woman's flute as well as other instruments to murder her doppelgänger. Ms. Yarrow had several identifying tattoos which Dr. Price carved from her skin. It was later discovered that Ms. Yarrow was three months pregnant and sadly her unborn child passed too.

Dr. Price then set the scene to frame the young woman, including planting evidence that suggested she was violent and jealous of her. She took photos of herself and her estranged husband and pressed Ms. Frank's fingers on them. She then marked up the photos, broke into Ms. Frank's home and put them up. When police found this, it was wrongly seen as clear evidence that Ms. Frank was unhinged.

Ms. Frank was promptly arrested at the scene of the fabricated crime scene. All the while, Dr. Price began living both on the streets and in shelters, assuming the life of Ms. Yarrow. As Denise had little connections due to her addiction, no one was suspicious of the swap.

Everyone else who knew Denise declined to comment. Her mother expressed remorse that they did not reconnect before her passing and stated how despite her troubles, she always truly loved her daughter.

"She will be missed forever and so will the grandchild I will never meet, never hold. I will be haunted with how they were taken from this Earth and can only hope that one day we will all be reunited."

Dr. Price's now ex-husband Mr. Sandoval, became suspicious that this situation wasn't what it seemed to be. He went to a cabin that they shared in Vermont. He told the Gazette, "I knew she would come back here if she was still alive. It was a special place for us when things were good."

Christian left a diary in the cabin, the final entry created to lure her back to him. He scribbled how badly he wanted to reconnect with his wife. He noted that having her gone made him realize how much he was missing her.

Dr. Price found the journal and contacted Mr. Sandoval. The police had tapped his line and were able to track her location.

She was taken into custody and will stand trial for the murder of Denise Yarrow and her unborn child, the assault on Ms. Frank, as well as a series of other charges. She will face life in prison at the trial. The date for the trial is unknown.

Previously, Isabella Frank had spent time in jail for the suspected murder of Danielle Price Sandoval. However, she has now been released. Ms. Frank is no longer a suspect and continues to live in the area. Her lawyer, Nicola McDermont, asks that everyone respects her privacy at this time as she needs to heal from this traumatic event.

This story is still unraveling. Check back with the Hamilton Gazette for continued updates.

Epilogue

1 year later

To say that an experience like this will change you is an understatement.

But I'm a Jersey Girl, so when I get pushed down, I flip you the bird and then come back stronger.

Right now, I am sitting on my balcony with a good book, a hot mug of coffee—and Christian sitting next to me. I feel the warm sun on my face and soak in how much simplicity fills my heart with joy.

My life has finally locked into a good rhythm. I met with a psychiatrist who properly diagnosed me and I've been on a course of medication that has greatly helped. I hope one day to be off of it—but that will come some day when I am ready.

With that, I've been able to find joy in all the things in my life both big and small. We planted a tree in Aubrey's memory. I've continued to play the flute, sometimes playing in the local park where the tree is planted. Before I start to play, I pluck weeds around the tree. While I play, it provides me shade.

Like a true friendship that Aubrey and I had, we help each other. My instrument fills the paths with music for joggers and families walking by to enjoy. As an added bonus, the tips people throw into my case are often enough to get a latte and scone afterwards.

And of course, all the people who supported me through the difficult times are still part of my support system.

I was broken. I still am broken to some extent.

I don't know if I will ever go back together, be whole but I know that I am in a better place because of my support system.

Talia and Lucas split up but we all remain friends. They spent many days speaking, crying, arguing, trying to figure out if they had a path forward. Mutually, they decided it was best to support each other as friends but not be romantically involved.

It is cheesy to say but the best thing to come out of this nightmare is my ideal partner, who is more perfect that I could have imagined. As a kid I thought I would need grand gestures to show love, a room filled with roses and candles or expensive dinners. What we have is so much better—a true understanding of the other person.

We disagree with respect and listen to the other person, trying to take in their point of view until we come to a mutual agreement. We support each other in all our endeavors, cheering for them at the high points and being a listening ear when things don't go how we expected. We appreciate each other and that is where true love blooms.

Christian turned to me and said, "It's a good day, Isa."

We've made a habit of doing this check in with each other at the beginning of the day. Given everything that has happened, we felt it was important to make sure the other person was doing okay mentally, emotionally, physically. It was these small moments that showed how much we cared for each other.

"It's a good day, Christian." I made eye contact with him as I said it so he knew I was being honest.

We moved to a small, extremely old house in Pennington. It was a fixer upper which was both a total headache and a nice distraction. Christian has tried to pick up some handyman skills to navigate all the little issues that keep popping up. Let's just say this isn't his strong suit and after watching him struggle for a few hours with something, I sneak off to call a proper handyman.

Our lives are much simpler now. Danielle had been in jail for the past thirteen months and would probably be there for the rest of her life. Once she was away, our anxiety went with it and we could focus on each other.

We began to prioritize our needs, our own mental health, self-care and being more consistent in our time together. Gone are the days of us yo-yoing in and out of each other's lives. Once things were stable, Christian proposed to me, promising that each day of our lives would be lived with kindness and care.

"We better get packing," he said, bending down to give me a quick kiss. As he leaned over me, I ran my fingers through his black hair, pausing at his neck and drawing him to me for a deeper kiss.

With that, we got up, holding hands and went inside to our bedroom. I slipped on my engagement ring which I kept on my nightstand. I rummaged through the bright pink beach bag doing a triple check—sunscreen, sunglasses, bathing suit and passport. Those were the essentials.

"I think I'm all set," I said to him.

"Oh, are you?" he teased, handing me the two guidebooks for Jamaica that I had forgotten to pack. I tossed them into my carry on.

"We can read these on the plane."

"Sure, we can check out all the places that we won't be going to." He winked at me and I laughed.

I smirked, understanding what he was getting at. We had booked an all-inclusive resort but probably wouldn't be leaving the bedroom often.

He came up to me and embraced me, his emerald eyes looking into my soul. "There was a point where I thought I'd never get to hold you again. Now I get to hold you all day every day."

I closed my eyes taking in the moment and giving thanks for feeling happiness once again.

Dear reader,

Thank you so much for taking a chance and reading my indie book! If you are anything like me, books can be an escape to another time and place and I hope this book provided that for you too. If you are interested in following my writing journey, please us the QR code to follow me.

Best,

    A.L.L.